Kristin B.

and Other Stories

Kristin B.

and Other Stories

Joseph Raffetto

NOOVELLA.COM

For my parents

Table of Contents

Young Scott & Zelda

Gatsby believed in the green light, the orgastic future that year by year recedes before us. It eluded us then, but that's no matter—tomorrow we will run faster, stretch out our arms farther.... And then one fine morning—

So we beat on, boats against the current, borne back ceaselessly into the past.

—F. Scott Fitzgerald, *The Great Gatsby*

I

PERHAPS I DESERVED TO DIE before my literary resurrection. Zelda flew too close to the sun, but she did not deserve to die by fire.

The door to the room that Zelda stayed in was locked and the window was bolted on the outside as the flames overwhelmed the mental hospital.

There are no second acts in American lives.

I have a precise and creative memory when it comes to events in my life, particularly my crackups. It was in 1917 at the St. Paul Country Club when I suffered my first.

In one corner, a group of boys were giving their attention to the dark-haired beauty—Ginevra King. They cut in to dance with her frequently.

It seemed to be an innocent and happy competition for everyone except me—a blond, lean, and almost girlishly pretty literary dandy. It was a tragedy and a comedy that Ginevra was no longer interested in me. I could not imagine losing her, as I observed the proceedings with both hands stuffed in my pockets. Alongside me was my boyhood pal, friendly-faced Tubby Washington.

My obsessive thoughts were interrupted by an athletic, exuberant, handsome youth named Reuben Warner. Reuben was everything I yearned to be. Because of Reuben, I was always the second-most popular boy in school in St. Paul. I indulged in the kind of hero worship I would continue to practice my entire life—with Princeton football players, Hemingway, and finally the studio executive Irving Thalberg, the inspiration for my unfinished novel, *The Last Tycoon*.

"Guess who wants to go riding with me?" Reuben asked.

"I knew it."

"Don't be jealous, Scott. You told me yourself it was all over between you two."

I glared at Reuben before marching onto the floor and cutting in on a boy who had just begun dancing with Ginevra. He seemed perturbed, but Ginevra mollified him by thanking him with a hand squeeze and a charming smile.

"Hello, Scott."

I ignored the indifference in her voice. She was a product of wealth and eastern finishing schools, so I respected her superiority. "After everything that's happened between us, you're still the most beautiful girl I'll ever know."

"You are such a nervous strain."

"My train leaves tomorrow morning."

There was a war going on, and I was being commissioned soon, but it was a daydream or abstraction that did not affect me personally in any way.

"I vaguely recall you mentioning something of the sort earlier this evening."

I ached for her and needed to think of another tactic as I saw an eager boy bumbling through other dancers to cut in. "After all we've been through, we should spend my last evening in St. Paul together," I said.

"I'm sorry. I'm riding with Reuben Warner in his new Stutz Bearcat tonight." Ginevra reached her hand out to the bumbler.

I crouched over the wheel of my parents' old Marmon. Tubby sat next to me, alternating looks between me as I drove too fast and the slick road in front of us.

"Slow down, Scott. Please."

I enjoyed ignoring him and sank my head against the steering wheel in torment. Tubby knocked the car out of gear. It slowed to a crawl, stopping in the middle of the street.

"Let me drive, Scott. You've had a few too many drinks."

"She crumpled me up and threw me over with an admirable complacence."

"She's not good enough for you."

"Not good enough? She's the most popular girl from Chicago to St. Paul."

"Perhaps, but poor boys shouldn't think of marrying rich girls."

Tubby's expression suggested he wished he had not spoken up. As much as I resented him saying it, I believed it was true.

"You're right. I'm not the sort of man she is looking for," I admitted, jumping out of the car.

"Where are you going? Scott! Come back."

"I'll write you from the front line."

Seeing me off at the train station the next day were my tired, proper father, my energetic, eccentric mother, and my fourteen-year-old sister.

It was a moment I dreaded. I was not close to my family and secretly fantasized that I was adopted and really the child of royalty.

My father was an easygoing Southern gentleman with fine manners and a loser's melancholy. My mother, on this occasion in an ensemble of mismatched clothes, often embarrassed me. She had been seen around town wearing two different shoes.

She began to fret, hugging me and refusing to let go. "My beautiful boy is going to war."

"Pray for my novel, Mother." I pulled away from her grip. "I'll write you as soon as I know where I'll be stationed."

"Good luck with your novel, Scott!" my sister yelled.

I smiled and waved enthusiastically; I was happy to be returning to New York to speak with Scribner about my novel and to Princeton to gather my belongings before I was stationed.

As I grew older, I became more estranged and detached from my family.

Family quarrels are bitter things. They don't go according to any rules. They're not like aches or wounds; they're more like splits in the skin that won't heal because there's not enough material.

Most infantrymen believed they were going to die at the front, although I never seriously thought I would be killed. I was more concerned with *The Romantic Egoist*, a coming-of-age novel combining everything I had written up to that point: poems, lyrics, and short stories.

Most of the literature professors during my time at Princeton possessed the distinct ability to make literature distasteful to young men. I only stayed in touch with one after I left—the brilliant Professor Gauss. It was thanks to his recommendation that I had the privilege of being invited to Scribner to discuss my unpublished first novel. As I entered, I felt dashing in my Brooks Brothers suit, but I was about to meet someone more dashing than I—the brilliant editor, Maxwell Perkins.

"I am favorably impressed with your talent. In fact, I've taken the liberty of discussing you with Mr. Scribner."

This was everything I'd lived for.

"I, like Mr. Scribner, was struck with its crudity and cleverness. Unfortunately, we do not feel it is ready for publication."

"I hoped to leave something behind in case I'm killed at the front."

"I hesitate to say this, but an editor here mentioned that as long as you're alive, it has literary value, but if you're killed, it will have commercial."

Maxwell and I observed a moment of silence before we both smiled.

"You have a tremendous gift, Scott," he said with sincerity. "I hope when you have a chance to rewrite your book, you will give us another opportunity to accept."

Life crushed down. Now, even literature had abandoned me. I had enlisted to save face because I had flunked out of Princeton. Instead of becoming a big shot on campus, I was going to be marching in army boots.

The previous summer, I had gone to Mass each Sunday and even considered becoming a priest. My inspiration for such heavenly thoughts was Monsignor Fay. He possessed the magic to turn Catholicism into a glorious, living organism, and he happened to be in New York. It was Fay I went to see after my disappointment in Maxwell Perkins's office.

A butler greeted me as I entered the large, luxurious residence that resembled the home of an old Stuart king. Fay, too stout for symmetry, practically an albino, and possessor of a high, shrill laugh, greeted me.

"My dear boy, my son." Fay led me to a high-backed chair. "I've been anxious to see you since your sudden departure from Princeton."

I frowned, disturbed by the reference to my school troubles.

Fay poured a glass of red wine and offered me a cigarette from a gold case.

"Thank you, Monsignor."

I paced back and forth.

"It can't be all that tragic, dear boy."

"It may seem petty, but my career at Princeton went up in smoke—all the councils, the clubs, the presidency of the musical comedy club, the honors that I worked so hard to achieve. Scribner only wants to publish me if I'm killed at the front. I've lost half my personality in the last six months."

"You've not lost anything too valuable, only a great amount of vanity, that's all." Fay refilled my glass. "What you need to do is the next thing." His grave, moonlike face gravitated toward me.

"The next thing?"

"The next thing will not arrive without struggle. You'll be extraordinary whatever your vocation proves to be—literature or something else. That's why I have taken you under my wing. I'm sure you would be much safer anchored to the church." Fay lifted the rosary beads hanging from his neck and handed them to me.

I wasn't able to think about what Fay said; I was in a youthful fog as I traveled to Princeton to await my commission into the army.

Two tall spires and then suddenly all around you spreads out the loveliest riot of Gothic architecture in America, battlement linked on to battlement, hall to hall, arch-broken, vine-covered—

luxuriant and lovely over two square miles of green grass. Here is no monotony, no feeling that it was all built yesterday at the whim of last week's millionaire; Nassau Hall was already thirty years old when Hessian bullets pierced its sides.

I threw open the door of my cottage flat and considered Bunny Wilson—my fellow editor of the Princeton paper and a future brilliant critic. "I want to be the greatest writer ever, don't you?"

"I don't possess your youthful enthusiasm." Bunny frowned and handed me a sealed envelope with a military logo.

I opened it. "Francis Scott Key Fitzgerald is to report to Leavenworth, Kansas, for officer's training…" I had read enough.

Bunny seemed to understand my sudden melancholy and wandered onto the balcony to view the grounds.

"Do you think the Germans will reach Paris?" I asked.

"I'm wagering they won't."

"There are ghosts everywhere already."

"The campus is crawling with them."

A manicured tennis court faced our flat. Instead of lobbing tennis balls on the grass courts, a group of eager and inept young men trained and marched, preparing to fight and perhaps to die in Europe.

$$II$$

THREE WEEKS OF PARTIES, letters, uniform fittings, and travel preceded my arrival at Leavenworth, Kansas.

It was a blue-eyed West Pointer—Captain Dwight D. Eisenhower—who caught me rewriting my novel behind my *Small Problems for Infantry* manual.

"You're unfit to command, Fitzgerald, you Ivy League sissy," Eisenhower's aide said to me.

It was true. I was a lousy officer, but I didn't mind. All my energy was focused on my novel. After a burst of furious editing, I re-sent *The Romantic Egoist* to Scribner, only to have them turn it down again, reminding me that my only hope of publication was dying in battle.

When my battalion was transferred to Montgomery, Alabama, I concentrated on my social life and often went to dances at a country club elevated by wooden pillars and protected by a hedge of orange trees.

I attended one particular dance with a new friend—Harvard man and fellow officer Joseph Devereux. We were excited by the spirit of our new companions: young officers, locals, and Southern belles, all dancing or planning some adventure.

On the verandah, couples whispered and flirted. Young Southerners and servicemen dotted the parking fields.

I had already had several romances in Montgomery, though none that blossomed into anything serious, when from across the club, a circle of laughing men parted and I spotted her, brighter than herself; her skin impeccable; straight, perfect nose, and round, kissable mouth.

"Who is that?"

"The local belle. Chaps from Alabama to Georgia are fighting over her," Joseph informed me.

I stared at this sun-drenched seventeen-year-old as she dazzled a group of admiring officers.

"You two look like you could be related."

"I have to meet her."

Zelda wrote later that I appeared to be as light as an angel as I floated up to her from across the dance floor on our first meeting.

"You're the most beautiful girl I've ever seen."

"Is that the line you use on us Southern girls?" She smiled as if she were delighted by my introduction.

"Is this dance taken?"

"Why, no. I don't believe it is."

The men grouped near Zelda murmured, perturbed that I had slipped through their ranks.

Zelda didn't seem to notice.

"What's your name?" I asked.

"What's yours?"

"Francis Scott Key Fitzgerald."

"Francis Scott Key wrote "The Star Spangled Banner." He was a Southerner."

"Yes—he's my great-uncle," I bragged.

Zelda didn't seem impressed and pouted. "Zelda Sayre. My mother read my name in a book. Zelda was queen of the gypsies."

She bit her lip as we danced.

"Could we meet later on the verandah?"

"I don't give late dates to fast workers," she said.

A stiff, dignified pilot with a mustache stepped in and tapped me on the shoulder.

"May I call on you?" I asked.

"Suit yourself."

I fell in love with her courage, her sincerity, and her flaming self-respect. And it's these things I'd believe in, even if the whole world indulged in wild suspicions that she wasn't all she should be. I love her and it is the beginning of everything.

Two days passed before I could get away and stand, along with twenty other servicemen, on the rattletrap bus that brought us into town. I took it all in easily—the blue sky, the outline of the surrounding forests, the meadows.

I found a cab to take me to Zelda's. The driver manipulated

a toothpick in his mouth as he examined me in the rear-view mirror.

"Six Pleasant Avenue? That's ole Judge Sayre's place."

"Judge Sayre?"

"Which Sayre are you calling on?"

"Zelda," I said, eager to admit it.

He chuckled. "She's a thoroughbred."

"No, she's the queen of the gypsies."

"Whatever you say, Lieutenant."

The Sayre home was a large, sunny, two-story white house with a long porch and a swing. I paid the driver, who seemed to appreciate my generous tip.

"Thank you, Lieutenant."

Zelda's stout and amicable mother, Minnie Sayre, appeared at the front door.

"My name is Scott..." I began.

"Why don't you wait on the swing, and I'll call her."

Zelda brushed by her mother. She was dressed casually, almost carelessly, in direct contrast to my pressed, tailored uniform. Zelda sniffed, acknowledging my cologne.

"What are you wearing?"

"Russian Leather. It's the fashion at Princeton."

"I approve."

With an air of nonchalance, Zelda led me to the swing at the end of the porch.

"We can sit out here, though there's no telling when Mama

might peep her head out...unfortunately," she added, under her breath.

A low rattle and hum interrupted us. "Come on," Zelda said, running into the front yard. I followed, and we craned our necks skyward. An airplane rumbled nearer and nearer before turning upside down over the Sayre house and departing, waving its wings.

"A friend of yours?"

"I reckon," she said.

Jellybean rode up on a motorbike. He perched his goggles on his head and gazed at the disappearing plane. "They sure do some crazy stunts to impress you."

Zelda swayed over to him. "Hey, how about a ride?"

"Hop on."

"I want to drive," Zelda said.

"Well, I guess that would be all right." He slid off his bike.

Zelda hopped on and revved the throttle.

Zelda circled me. "I just want to show the lieutenant a little southern hospitality."

Jellybean scratched his head. "I guess that would be all right."

I hopped on the motorbike.

"We won't be long!" Zelda told him.

We buzzed down the quiet street. Unsure if I should place my hands on Zelda's slender waist, I tried to balance without touching her. I noticed her smiling, as if she approved of my self-conscious manners.

Taking her eyes off the road, she turned to speak to me. "I

hope it doesn't offend your wealthy Princeton sensibilities to be driven around by Miss Alabama Nobody."

"Zelda!"

She headed straight for an oak tree, then veered and avoided it at the last moment, hopped the curb, and drove through somebody's flowerbed. In high spirits the entire time, Zelda pulled back over the front yard onto the street. I gripped her and hung on.

Later, we lounged in a languid field below the dreamy skies of Montgomery. We shared and puffed on the same cigarette. The motorbike lay nearby.

"When I'm out of the army I'm living in Manhattan. I'm going to be a great novelist. The finest editor in New York thinks so."

This was the first time I realized how jealous Zelda could be. "I'm multi-talented. I paint, dance, and write," she pouted.

"You write?"

"Love letters and my diary."

"I'm sure your diary would be a bestseller."

"Maybe I'll let you read it, if I ever fall in love with you."

I smiled. "I'd like you to read my novel before I'm killed at the front."

"Does that mean you're in love with me?"

"Why do you think I'm stationed here?" I said, happy to give her the satisfaction of flattery.

I had no idea at the time how deep Zelda's desire to be the

center of attention was. She cracked while in a mania to become a professional ballerina. She was never going to be one; in fact, she was always going to be a first-rate person but a third-rate artist. She never accepted that she was not on my level.

Jellybean was sipping lemonade with Zelda's sister and Minnie when we returned. I pushed the motorbike as Zelda strolled confidently alongside me.

"I reckon it's out of gas or something," Zelda drawled.

"I guess if my daddy was a judge, I'd be a law unto myself, too."

"Would you care to supper with us, Jellybean?" Zelda asked. "You're welcome."

"I'm going for a swim. Thanks all the same." He didn't seem upset as he ambled by Zelda and took the handlebars from me.

"Suit yourself." She shrugged.

I nodded goodbye to the easygoing Southerner.

At the Sayre dinner table, I was seated across from Minnie and Zelda's attractive older sister, Rosalind.

Judge Sayre occupied the head. His black-gray hair and little round glasses accentuated his seriousness. He barely acknowledged me.

"You went to Princeton and are interested in becoming a writer?" Rosalind asked, with a slight mocking tone of disapproval.

"He is a writer, Rosalind. *Is*," Zelda corrected.

"Scribner is interested in publishing my novel."

"Scott is going to live in New York City," Zelda said.

"It's nothing at all like what you imagine," Rosalind told her.

"Lieutenant Fitzgerald has told me all about it." Zelda stuck her tongue out, then smiled at me.

It never took Zelda long to become bored, so she decided to provoke her father.

"Take a gander at the Judge's plate," she said. "He loathes his food touching."

The food on his plate was organized in isolated sections.

"You should have seen the Judge this afternoon after Joe Ingram checkmated him. He just stared at that old board for hours. I declare, you would have thought he had lost a battle in the war," Zelda said.

Her father gripped his knife.

"Dinner is delicious, Mrs. Sayre," I said.

"You don't supper like this up north, do you?" Mrs. Sayre asked.

"No."

"Pass the peas, please, Lieutenant," Mrs. Sayre alliterated.

"The Judge's idea of a night on the town is sitting in his old library, reading stuffy old law books. A visit to a bootlegger might loosen him up. Then maybe he'd take mama out dancing and shake some of his old cobwebs loose."

Her father exploded. "You little hussy!" He lunged, gripping his fork, but she was too quick for him. She jumped up with unrestrained laughter. He took off after her and chased her with a vengeance. "I'll teach you to talk to your father that way."

He was surprisingly fast, but not quick enough to catch the screaming and high-spirited Zelda. They went round and round the table. Mrs. Sayre and Rosalind continued to eat as if nothing were out of the ordinary. He became winded and returned to his seat. Zelda waited a moment, and then slipped into her chair next to him.

"Would you care for grits, Lieutenant?" Mrs. Sayre asked.

Zelda and I loved for something to happen, whether it was hi-jinks or confrontation. She often provoked me—once into fighting a bouncer, who shoved me halfway across the room, knocking down tables and chairs. The next morning, our friend Lawton Campbell came to see me in bed. My head was bandaged, one eye almost closed and black. It was the first of many reckless episodes.

Zelda and I wandered outside. It was a peaceful, firefly-filled evening. She studied the stars.

"I'll be eighteen next week. Mama is telling me to marry a boy whose daddy owns half of Alabama."

"What do you want to do?"

Zelda smiled abstractly. "It's difficult to be two simple people at once—one who wants to keep all the nice old things and be loved and safe and protected, and one who wants to feel that her life is her own."

Zelda searched my face with a strange yearning that I now understand was a tortured intelligence and alienation. People didn't realize how alone Zelda was. There was never a time in her life when she had a close friend or confidante. I didn't realize this at the time and learned later that there was a history of suicide and mental illness in her family. These were secrets the Sayres kept from me.

"Why can't you be both?" I asked.

"It's impossible, I reckon."

"Which are you now?"

"I'm safe and protected."

"It seems your life is your own."

"You're not the only one who wants to live life on a grand scale."

III

MY SHINING MOMENT during training in Alabama came while several men were shooting mortars, one after the other, across the Tallapoosa River. *Bang. Bang. Bang.* It was probably obvious in my expression that I found this exercise distasteful. As the men began to reload, I noticed a barge full of troops and horses crossing the river.

"He has that barge packed," I said, to no one in particular.

"We're ready, sir," a red-haired corporal reported.

"From a distance, it appears to be sinking."

"It is sinking, sir," the red-haired corporal said.

"Everyone to the river—double time!" I ordered.

The men and I raced down a winding, dusty trail that led to the dock. I ran as fast as I could, but was still one of the last to reach the shore. By the time I arrived, some of the men were panicked, as they and their horses splashed into the water.

A nervous officer yelled, "Some of the men can't swim, Lieutenant!"

I signaled that I understood. "If you can swim, strip down," I ordered. "We'll all need to go at least once."

I singled out the red-haired corporal. "Return to camp and bring back men who can swim and a medic."

Later that week, after sharing my military training exploits with Zelda, we went for a swim. As I climbed and kicked pebbles and rocks into a swimming hole, I glanced down, nervous because I had never jumped from such a height.

"I've been looking forward to this all day," Zelda said. She set herself and pushed off—an effortless, graceful dive with very little splash.

I gulped, arms folded across my white torso.

"Well, what are you waiting for?" Zelda yelled up.

"I wanted to be sure you were not in my line," I said. I took a deep breath. It was a brave dive, but not nearly as graceful as Zelda's. I flinched a little before I splashed in, but when I popped up, I was proud, eagerly searching for Zelda.

"You might as well have not dived if you were going to flinch," she said.

"What do you mean?" I said.

"It ruins everything when you flinch," she explained.

I wondered later if Zelda's uncompromising personality was the root of her illness. The doctor at La Paix suggested Zelda's schizophrenia would have eventually claimed her anyway, though my drinking and weakness probably accelerated it. I never accepted the accusation that I was to blame by the Sayres and others.

Army life droned on, with drilling and marching and endless repetition. I dreamed of Zelda. When I received a leave, eager to make up for my flinch, I led her up the steps to the well-lit club. When we entered the hall, only the band was present.

"This is eerie. Cars are outside but everyone's hiding. I'm going to find out what they're all doing," Zelda said.

I touched her arm, and enjoyed her perplexed expression.

"Happy birthday." I nodded to the band.

A jazzy rendition of "Happy Birthday to You" broke the silence as floods of Zelda's acquaintances, old and new, poured out of the back rooms. Joseph and an attractive, auburn-haired local, Eleanor Browden, rolled out a birthday cake with eighteen candles. The proper-looking Mary Lou stood next to Eleanor. Zelda's smile wandered across the room as she bent over, surprised, and leaped in the air.

"Eleanor, you knew about this the whole time! I'm going to tar you," Zelda said.

"It was Lieutenant Fitzgerald's doing. I just learned about it myself," Eleanor replied.

Zelda rotated to see everyone around her.

"Blow them out."

"Now we'll see how many boyfriends Zelda really has," Eleanor joked.

"Better find some more candles," Mary Lou snickered.

Zelda shot Mary Lou a nasty glare, then exhaled a happy breath across the candles. She stuck her tongue out at Mary Lou.

Much wilder than the rest, Zelda and I danced the Charleston, the Shimmy, the Black Bottom. I was said to be dashing, but inaccurate; Zelda's dancing was exuberant and smooth. Later, I carved "Scott + Zelda" on the top step of the club with a pocketknife.

In the parking lot, Zelda, Joseph, Eleanor, Mary Lou, and I passed a bottle of gin around. Our faces exuded a healthy gleam from the dancing.

Eleanor tried a tiny sip. Joseph and I took big swigs, as did Zelda, who passed the bottle.

"No, thank you," Mary Lou said.

"Have you ever drunk before?" Zelda asked.

"Of course not."

"Well, how do you know what it's like if you don't try?"

Mary Lou glanced around for some guidance.

"Don't be such a girl. Have some guts about you," Zelda demanded, pushing the bottle on her.

In town after the party, Zelda and I guided the giddy, drunk Mary Lou up through her front yard.

When the porch light popped on, we were arm in arm as we weaved up the front steps.

We dropped Mary Lou and raced to leap the fence and crouch down, unable to stop laughing as her father discovered his daughter.

"Hi, Daddy! Where's the party?"

The moon shed soft light through the car window at Boodler's Point.

Zelda gripped my feverish neck. She couldn't seem to get enough as I sweated and grinded on top of her.

Zelda's lovely, perfect skin glistened.

I ejaculated.

I lifted up off of her and fell back on the seat. She understood, I thought, and continued to lie there, catching her breath. Her rich, blonde hair lay tangled over her cheeks.

Although I was not present for the conversation the next day, Zelda gave a detailed account in her book, *Save Me the Waltz*, which I edited heavily to make publishable. The Judge was furious about the night's escapades. Minnie stood protectively over Zelda.

"I tell you, I will not have my daughter's name bandied about the street corner."

"Judge, she's hardly out of high school," Mrs. Sayre said.

"Minnie, please! Joe Ingram told me his daughter was brought home scandalously intoxicated, and she admitted that Zelda gave her the bottle."

"She didn't have to drink it. It's not my fault she can't handle her liquor," Zelda argued.

"There's going to be no more celebrations for you, young lady. You're staying home until you've gained some common sense."

Later that day, in Zelda's room, Minnie voiced the Sayre family position.

"Baby, a young man needs to be able to support you, and honey, you need lots of support."

"Money isn't everything, Mama."

"Baby, he's charming, but he didn't graduate, he's a writer, he's a Catholic, and he drinks."

"Mama, it's just personal."

"Don't be too personal. You and he can't afford it."

"He's serving our country, Mama. What's he supposed to do? Start a business and make a zillion dollars on the side?" Zelda was indignant and began to climb out the window on the second story to meet me. Minnie handed her a sweater.

The twilight cast mysterious shadows and patches of light on the lush countryside and river as Zelda and I strolled, holding hands, amid a chorus of crickets.

"According to the poet Keats, you and I should marry," I said.

"Why, you're an educational feature. An overture to romance, which no girl should do without."

She broke away and wandered a step ahead. "I'm just teasing. You should know how I feel about you," she offered. Zelda picked a flower and kneeled in front of me. She smelled it and held it out for me to smell as well.

"Does that mean you'll wait for me when I'm sent to the fighting?" I asked.

"The papers say they're going to sign the armistice any day."

"I'm scheduled to leave for the transport in Long Island next week."

"Scott, I can't wait for anyone."

IV

THE 67TH INFANTRY was being sent over. I had been having a wonderful time in Montgomery. I resented being in the army and being sent to fight a war that had nothing to do with me.

From inside a train filled with soldiers wearing their overseas caps, I gazed out at Zelda for what could have been the last time. "I love you," I mouthed.

Zelda repeated the words, "I love you."

A week later, on a dreary morning, I marched—along with the entire 67th Infantry—aboard the transport. A heavy fog was almost as thick as rain.

A grim grayness penetrated me as well as the rest of the battalion, when General Ryan appeared on the bow, rising above the gray monumental hull.

"I have some bad news, men—we're not going to sail today as planned. I know how anxious you are to get over to the action and how disappointed you must be, but they signed the armistice," the general said.

It began to dawn on me as well as everyone else that the war was over. The word "armistice" buzzed through the troops.

"They signed the armistice."

"We're not going," I said.

"We're free."

"We're not going over."

Joseph and I jumped up and down as men danced on deck, tossing caps into the fog.

Later, the barracks were filled with happy conversations and homesick soldiers. I sat on a cot next to Joseph, who was writing a letter to his parents.

"The entire world is celebrating, and we're cooped up a half hour outside New York. It's not fair," I said.

"It's the army," Joseph replied.

"Nobody's watching, Joseph. Let's sneak into the city for the night. They'll never miss us."

"We're supposed to re-camp back to Montgomery any minute."

"They've been saying that for two weeks."

"I've made it this far. I don't want to end my military career with a court martial."

"You only live once."

"That's my point, old man."

I felt free, free of the restraints of society, family, and the military.

I was within and without, simultaneously enchanted and repelled by the inexhaustible variety of life.

Outside the barracks, I sneaked behind a freight train. Unbeknownst to the chattering MPs, I crouched and tiptoed to the other freight. I waited, eager to be enjoying the celebrations I was sure were going on at Princeton and in Manhattan.

I started to make a dash for it, but a group of MPs appeared. I scurried back behind the freight train. I heard voices around the opposite end. I was in the middle. The voices became louder. I circled the freight car and kept walking between them. I turned back. They were talking and evidently never noticed me skip away.

Before the parties and celebrations, I went to see Monsignor Fay. He was a surrogate father and my last tenuous link to God and religion.

As Fay coughed again and again, I waited for him to recover.

"I should be ecstatic that you didn't get sent over, except I'm not sure which side of the Atlantic could be more dangerous," Fay warned.

I had no idea what he was talking about.

Fay used a handkerchief to pat the perspiration off his forehead. "Yes, you have given me a great deal to worry about. You are making a tragic mistake if you think you can be romantic without religion."

Zelda! He was talking about Zelda. "Oh, but it is romantic. She's honest and courageous and beautiful. I'd rather have died in Europe than live without her."

Fay sighed. "My dear boy. Beware of losing yourself in the personality of another being, man or woman. It's fortunate that, because of the calamitous state of your finances, you will be unable to marry in haste and repent in leisure."

Fay, of course, was right. I needed an anchor. I realized it then. I realized it again more than a decade later, when I was penniless and drinking forty beers a day. Somehow, I never found one.

After I left Fay, I found a wild celebration. I spotted my Princeton pal and fraternity brother, Ludlow Fowler, waiting for me in a relatively quiet corner of the bar near a window that overlooked the street below.

"By God, old man, I heard you were overseas," Ludlow said.

We shook hands with the Princeton low swoop.

"If they had signed the armistice a day later, I'd be there now cleaning up the mess."

"What bum luck you missed seeing any action," Ludlow said.

This became a sore topic that plagued me for the rest of my life. The war was the seminal event of my generation, and I missed it. Hemingway used to say war was a writer's greatest subject.

"I've fallen in love. By God, I'm in love, Ludlow."

"Let's drop by the club, and you can tell me all about it."

"That would be grand."

The next day, it occurred to me that I should call camp and see if I was missed. A nasal-toned corporal explained to me that the 67th Infantry was on its way to Montgomery via Washington.

"My company has retrained back to Montgomery without me," I told Ludlow.

"When did they leave?" Ludlow seemed calm.

"A half hour ago."

"They can put you in for desertion, old man."

"Can you get me to Pennsylvania Station?"

"I can."

Ludlow maneuvered someone's new Ford, weaving in and out of traffic and beeping the horn. A crowd of immigrants scattered as we screeched around a slow-moving Model T.

The hectic trip ended when Ludlow skidded to a stop in front of the station. His briefcase flew off the seat and fell at my knees.

"May I borrow this?" I asked.

"You may."

Ludlow popped it open and deposited its contents before handing it to me.

"I'll write."

"From the stockade."

I immediately found the nearest railroad official, a tall man with a bushy mustache. I tried to appear sharp and rigid, with a soldier's disciplined manner.

"Sir, I've been entrusted with confidential papers for General J.A. Ryan. I will need a train car immediately if I'm to meet him at Washington Station."

"What sort of papers?"

"Papers that can neither be trusted to the mails nor delayed an instant."

"Yes, of course."

I'm not sure he completely believed me, but he gave me a plush private compartment, where I enjoyed a newspaper and a cup of tea.

I arrived at the station before my battalion did. I shared a bench and waited with two attractive women. When my battalion's train car puffed in, it was packed with soldiers. A few in the sparse crowd outside began waving flags and cheering the troops.

I rose. "It was a pleasure sitting with you ladies," I said.

"It was delightful, Lieutenant. We are so proud of you, even if you didn't get any closer to the Germans than we did," one of them said.

Another reference to my nonparticipation overseas pricked me, but I stood and bowed gracefully and made my way to the train.

"Fitz. Fitz," Joseph hissed at me from a window.

He appeared tired and cramped, sitting next to a bulky soldier. I ambled up to him.

"Where the devil have you been? I've been worried sick about you."

"Has anyone noticed me missing?"

"I don't think so."

Back at Camp Sheridan, I was immediately called in to see General J.A. Ryan. The general, with whom I had never spoken, kept twisting his mustache as he scrutinized me.

"Fitzgerald, I value your style," he said, for no reason I understood. "You're a young man of some education."

"Thank you, sir."

"We also don't know what to do with you at this point, so I'm making you my new aide-de-camp," he said.

"Thank you, sir. You can depend on me."

"Dismissed, Lieutenant."

The irony warmed my heart as I contemplated my promotion and my imminent discharge from the army. I was outside the general's office when the red-haired corporal handed me a telegram that read:

Monsignor Fay died five P.M. Friday of pneumonia Funeral ten o'clock Our Lady of Lourdes New York City Come if possible

I was grieved by the loss of a man who I admired and who had once awakened a sense of spirituality in me, but most of all he was a father figure who cared about me. When I was able to get away, I went straight to Zelda's, only to spot her on the porch with the dark-haired football star, Perry Adair. I continued past the Sayre home to inspect the situation. Perry and Zelda sat close on the swing, evidently enjoying each other's company. When I saw that Perry was holding her hand, I tore out of the neighborhood.

I stopped at the local Baptist church, which was very different from the ornate Catholic ones I was used to. It didn't matter; there was a cross up there, and I went inside and began to pray for Fay, but I couldn't concentrate. A streak of sunlight shone through the open side door as several rather dreary-looking folks passed. One woman hummed to herself as she watered flowers. Fay was gone, and I felt a gnawing emptiness that I believed only Zelda could fill. I rose and hurried out.

I drove around for an hour or so before I confronted Zelda on the porch.

"How do you expect me to feel?" I asked her.

"I have to do something, or I'd just sit here and stagnate. It doesn't mean I love you any less," Zelda argued.

"What if I kissed another girl?"

"You can if you want, and I'd know you still loved me."

"I want to marry you," I stammered.

"The war's over, Scott. I have to be realistic. How would we live? I can't be shut away in a little flat. There would be nothing for me to do but think about pots and kitchens and brooms. You'd hate me in a narrow atmosphere. I'd make you hate me. I wouldn't be the Zelda you love." Her face radiated innate honesty.

That evening Minnie and Rosalind sat on the sofa, watching Zelda and me roast marshmallows in the fireplace. The scene was mellow and quiet except for our intimate giggles and whispers.

"She's awful to any suitable suitor who calls," I heard Rosalind say.

Zelda and I set down the marshmallow tongs.

"Scott and I are going for a stroll," Zelda announced.

"Put your coat on, baby, or you'll catch your death of cold," Minnie said.

"We're not going far," Zelda said.

"Good night." I smiled.

Zelda tried to keep from laughing, pushing me out of the library.

She climbed the shingles and vines that grew up the side of the house. She looked down at me and smiled. I followed.

Zelda's room was all white and surprisingly spare: cotton drapes, an armoire, and a bed. It resembled a hospital.

From the small, cream-colored armoire, Zelda dug out her old sketches. She drew with a gifted, hasty hand—ballerinas, landscapes, and self-portraits. She flipped through them one by one, until she presented me with her diary.

"You'll know everything there's to know about me," she said.

"You already know everything there is to know about me."

"Not everything."

She pulled off her sweater. She was not wearing a bra. Her lovely, golden, perfect, eighteen-year-old body....

Less than six or seven years later, after betrayals, abortions, and suicide attempts, Zelda tried to destroy my manhood by viciously attacking my sexual proclivity, saying I could never satisfy a woman. I confided in Hemingway. He exploited it later. I think he had it in for me ever since Gertrude Stein claimed people would be reading me long after Hemingway and the rest of our contemporaries were gone.

I was honorably discharged from the US Army and semi-engaged to Zelda.

"All aboard," the conductor called.

It appeared I was one of the few passengers on this run. I was dressed in my Brooks Brothers suit, appearing as sharp in my civilian clothes as I did in my army uniform.

"It won't be long before I send for you," I promised.

"As soon as you are able," Zelda said.

"Then we'll be together forever."

We both wanted more than middle-class life could offer. That liberal world Zelda and I desired was now mine to create.

I had to find a place to live in New York. I began by looking at a spacious room with a magnificent view of Central Park. I intended to rent it, until a cosmopolitan man handed me the lease, and I learned I could not afford it.

In the doorway of a nice apartment, a landlady quoted rent prices out of my range.

The next drizzling day, a man in a T-shirt showed me an average, run-down apartment. He asked for more than I could afford. I turned and exited past the children who were playing in front.

Finally, I followed an overdressed woman up a peeling, gray-walled flight of stairs to a drab room. The landlady spread out her arms proudly and said, "Here it is." I signed the lease. Later that night, I wrote this letter:

Dear Zelda:

Found knockout little apartment Reasonable rates. I feel sure of your love. Everything is possible – I am in land of ambition and success and my only hope and faith is that my darling heart will be with me soon.

In the grinding hiss of the subway car the following day, a scruffy wino's puffy left eye was closed. A large, sweating woman messily ate something I didn't recognize. I decided to look at nothing at all.

Carrying Ludlow's briefcase, I hustled into the *New York Times* office. A busy editor with his sleeves rolled up leafed through my stories. He did not seem particularly impressed.

"Two plays that were produced for charity before you were sixteen?"

"Yes."

"Big shot in college, literary magazine, and musical comedies."

"Presently, I have a novel that Scribner is considering."

"Kid, I get college geniuses in here every day looking for a job. You probably have some talent, but you're a dime a dozen to me."

On the street, I marched to a trashcan and flung my list of places to work into it.

American flags blanketed Times Square as bands marched out a vibrant beat, young girls twirled batons, and airplanes dropped ticker tape. Thick crowds lined the streets to get a glimpse of the returning heroes.

Ludlow and I made our way through the parade, until Ludlow spotted a dark-haired friend named Porter Gillespie, who had been saving a place for us.

"Scott Fitzgerald—Porter Gillespie: Princeton, sixteen," Ludlow introduced us. "This is the man I was talking about," Ludlow said to Porter.

Porter and I shook with the Princeton low swoop.

"Porter was telling me of an opportunity that may be in your field."

"Ludlow informed me of your plight. I was in the same position you are three months ago when I stumbled into an advertising agency out of sheer desperation. Are you interested in copy writing?" Porter asked.

"No."

"Could be promising," Ludlow suggested.

"They need a light verse man at the Barron Collier agency. Ludlow has told me a little bit about you, and with a good word, they might give a new man a chance. It may be hack work, but it pays the rent."

"I'm interested."

"I'll speak to them. You might be in luck," Porter said.

I peered through a pair of binoculars at the battle-hardened veterans parading by. "Look! Look at that!"

Several of the troops who trained on the tennis courts at Princeton marched our way. One of them did not have a leg.

"Bravo, old boy! Bravo," Ludlow shouted.

Ludlow and I choked up and wildly applauded.

My heart sank, knowing that I should have been there.

The following Tuesday, a kind, Mr. Collier at Barron Collier examined my resume. The sound of typing from the secretarial pool and a yawning older artist added to my sense of slow torture.

"A Princeton man. I'm sure you have potential. I'll start you off at ninety dollars a month." Apparently pleased, he shook my hand.

As I wrote in my short story, "May Day," on one memorable evening during this period, Porter and I stole black-and-white "IN" and "OUT" door signs. This was just after we were kicked out of a dance at the Plaza Hotel. We were drunk and becoming drunker, bottles of champagne in hand.

"All I've written is 'I'll keep you clean in Muscateen' for some steam cleaners in Muscateen, Iowa," I said.

"I'd have my shirts starched there," Porter said. "Doesn't matter tonight. Tonight you're the finest young writer in New York."

"The world."

"The world."

I toasted Porter's glass and enjoyed the champagne.

"What happened to your girl?" I asked.

Porter checked his pockets as if she might be in one. He did not find his date, but he did find his cigarettes. He lit one for each of us.

"Doesn't matter. Spoiled. Spoildest darn girl I ever met. I'm leaving her," he puffed.

"Good for you," I said, having learned that Zelda had recently accepted three separate dates to the Georgia Tech prom.

At six in the morning, Porter and I, fueled by another bottle of champagne, skipped arm in arm down Fifth Avenue.

"We want breakfast and liquor," I repeated over and over.

"Breakfast and liquor," Porter said.

"That's logical."

We approached Childs Restaurant, a seemingly quiet place to have breakfast.

Standing outside, I unbuttoned my coat and revealed the "IN" sign that I had stolen from the Plaza. Porter had the "OUT" sign inside his coat.

"These are very rare and valuable signs," I said.

"Probably come in handy."

I opened the door. "After you, Mr. Out."

"Thank you, Mr. In."

A representative mixture of the gayest of Broadway was here, although there were a couple of drab, mousy figures quietly pressed alongside the pale walls.

I mixed eggs, ketchup, and hash browns in someone's derby. I handed the derby to Porter, who passed it along, and it ended up with a tall gentleman who put it on his head, causing a chorus girl to break into a hysterical chortle.

The room was full of sudden bursts of revelry and bawdy behavior. I approached a group of young men and women with whom I was acquainted. I ignored their protests and stepped, a little wobbly, onto their table, causing them to shuffle their plates to keep me from stepping on their breakfast.

"I want to make a speech," I said.

No one really complained. Though several people hurled catcalls and wadded-up napkins at me, most appeared amused.

"You have to understand that this establishment only seems to curve because I'm drunk...and when I'm straight, I'm going to write about you and you and you and you...about all of you. We'll all be famous..."

The tall gentleman got the attention of several waiters. He pointed his long finger at Porter and me.

"Sir, you must come down from the table and get out," a waiter said.

"Nobody tells F. Scott Fitzgerald to get out."

I jumped down and the waiter chased me around the table. He wouldn't have caught me, but two waiters who arrived on the scene took hold of me from behind.

The Childs crowd minded its own business until I was being escorted to the door. They booed the infringement on the gay, anything-goes atmosphere.

"You can't throw him out; he's my friend," Porter said aristocratically, with no intention of coming to my rescue. "And he hasn't paid his bill."

The waiters heard this and looked at one another, then let me loose. I struck an air of dignified respect.

After I paid our bill, Porter and I, armed with two more bottles of champagne, stumbled down the street. "Imagine anyone objecting to us having champagne for breakfast," Ludlow said.

"Mortifying. That's the word. Mortifying."

We weaved across the street from a Catholic church. The congregation milled about outside, trying to ignore us.

Annoyed at this slight, I rolled a bottle in their direction. It trickled against the curb. Their pious and judgmental manners insulted me. I took Porter's bottle and flung it as hard as I could, shattering it in the street. I gawked at the shocked churchgoers and staggered away.

Sometimes I don't know whether I'm real or whether I'm a character in one of my novels.

At my depressing apartment, I labored up the stairs, past the landlady.

"Good morning," she said.

"Good morning."

The landlady leaned back in her doorway, showing off her dramatic curves as she handed me my mail.

Inside, I ripped open a letter from Zelda and wandered into

the middle of my messy kitchen. Distraught and impaired, I passed out.

At work the next day, I arrived a half-hour late and immediately entered Mr. Collier's office. I stood, tapping my foot, before his desk. I sensed the pressure of possible failure.

"There's a family emergency that requires my presence. I have to leave right away. It's terribly important that I be there," I said.

"I hope everything's okay."

"I do, too."

I arrived in Montgomery and stepped off the train. I didn't see Zelda until I wiggled my way through the other passengers. I found her, dressed in white and calm.

At the Sayre house, Zelda and I sat close, rocked by the porch swing.

"I miss you," I said, for the second time.

Perhaps touched by my sincerity, she glanced down at our interlaced fingers, then up to my yearning eyes.

A car drove by and the horn blew. Two young men waved and shouted "Zelda!" Our romantic moment was disrupted.

"Do other boys come and see you often?"

"Why, of course they do—all the time. I wrote that they do," Zelda said, as if she were annoyed I would bring that up.

I sat, pensive and jealous. "Marry me. We'll take a few years of hard knocks, but we'll be happy in New York."

"We agreed to wait until we're ready. Now sit back and relax.

You're tired and tense from overwork."

"It's only when I'm away from you that I'm tense."

"I wish you didn't have to leave so soon."

"I could stay a couple more days."

"Won't they miss you at work?"

"The stupidities of advertising will survive without me."

Something about Zelda shifted, as if she realized for the first time how distasteful my work was to me. I attempted to cover up the mistake.

"You're right. Most people would feel lucky to be in my shoes."

Advertising is a racket, like the movies and the brokerage business. You cannot be honest without admitting that its constructive contribution to humanity is exactly minus zero.

I certainly didn't feel lucky when I returned to New York. I immediately got horribly drunk, but somehow managed to make it to work the next day. I don't know why I went in, because all I could do was bury my face in my hands at my desk. "Water..." I mumbled, rose delirious, and made my way to the cooler, where I ran into Mr. Collier.

He handed a glass to me, and I guzzled it down before suffering a coughing fit.

"You look terrible. I hope everything is all right with your family."

I guzzled more water. "I didn't go to see them."

"Then where did you go?"

"Montgomery, Alabama—to see a girl."

"I see," he said, with a dumb and confused expression.

"You've been more than kind, but I can't adjust to the business routine. I don't deserve to work here."

"Go home and get some sleep, Fitzgerald. You don't know what you're saying."

At my apartment, the nosy landlady, in a low-cut, low-class dress, greeted me in her doorway.

"You sure are a pretty boy. It's all right if you meet a girl and want to bring her up to your room. I wouldn't mind." The landlady's body language suggested she wouldn't mind being that girl.

"Why would I do that? I have a girl. She's waiting for me in Alabama."

When I saw the Montgomery postmark and Zelda's handwriting, I rushed upstairs past the landlady.

I slit open the envelope and dumped out a pin. It had been addressed to me, but the letter was to a wealthy, handsome Georgia boy Zelda had gone to a prom with. She evidently had a delightful time and accepted his pin, which was tantamount to being in a relationship. She was returning the pin to him, since she was engaged to me, though she didn't mention that in the letter.

I was furious at her insensitivity and carelessness and took a huge swipe at my manuscript, sending it flying. This was one of the few times I had touched my writing since I returned to New York.

The following morning, I popped my head into Mr. Collier's office.

"Can you spare a moment, sir?"

He seemed to sense something coming. My hand beat against my thigh with impatient energy.

"What is it, Fitzgerald?"

"I need four days off. It's an emergency that can't be helped."

"Why, you just had a vacation."

"I have to have another. It's beyond my control."

"You're not hired here as a traveling salesman."

He needed to raise his voice because I was already halfway out the door.

Two days later, Zelda and I sat on the sofa in the library. A fan hummed. She bit her nails. I wrote about this meeting in my short story, "The Sensible Thing."

"What difference does it make if it was a mix-up?"

"I know it was inexcusable, but I'm not going to fold my hands and sit home every night."

"You mean you think I'll never have enough money to marry you."

Zelda snapped, saying I was jumping to conclusions.

I accused her of jumping to conclusions that I was jumping to conclusions.

She bit her lip.

"I want to marry you now more than anything," I said.

"Are you ready to marry me?"

The humming fan began to drive me wild. "It's like a clock ticking away all the time I'll be with you," I said.

I flipped it off and leaned into her, unable to control my compulsive love.

She turned away and gazed out the window. "It must be the hottest day of the year, and there's nothing to do." Zelda faced me. "There's no use going on. I think we both can sense it."

"What do you mean?" I asked, knowing exactly what she meant.

"You hate the advertising business and you'll never do well in it."

"If you'd marry me and take a chance with me, I could make good at anything, but not while I'm worrying about you down here."

"Scott, I can't marry you, and it's not because you're poor. It doesn't seem to be the...the sensible thing."

Zelda being sensible might seem ironic, but she was often sensible in surprising ways.

I hovered desperately over Zelda and accused her of having an affair.

"There's nobody else—you know that."

I attempted to kiss Zelda into marrying me. She turned her head, pushed me away, and remained hunched over in her seat. Then we both began crying.

"Don't you see what losing you means to me? I could be a success if I only had you by my side."

Zelda stared at her boots so she didn't have to witness my pathetic self-pity.

"I'll leave if you want me to," I said, realizing that I had betrayed my dignity.

"Perhaps it's best you should."

I kneeled in front of Zelda. "This is all a mistake. Let's start the day over and forget any of this happened. I didn't mean to rush you, honest I didn't."

Minnie entered the room with two lemonades. "I thought you two might like some lemonade."

Zelda rushed out.

"Is there something the matter, Scott?" Minnie asked.

"I'm going away, Minnie."

Minnie didn't bat an eyelash. She left the lemonade, and then the room. Zelda returned, detached and cool. "I've ordered a taxicab. We can drive around until the next train leaves," she said.

As our marriage disintegrated, Zelda asked:

What is our marriage anyway? It's been nothing but a constant battle ever since I can remember.

She was right; it was a constant battle from the very beginning.

In the cab, I became more and more miserable. I turned to Zelda, who just stared straight ahead. The familiar cab driver kept glancing at me in the mirror.

At the station, I faced Zelda for what I thought could be the last time.

"We can write each other," she said.

"No, I couldn't stand that."

She bit her lip.

One thousand miles north of Zelda, I drowned my sorrows while the rest of New York celebrated military victory and an economic boom.

I unsteadily tilted a drink to my lips. I survived the war, but I might not survive losing Zelda. Somehow I found myself lying on the floor, staring at the ceiling. I could hear Ludlow and Porter talking above me.

"He's taking this pretty hard," Ludlow said.

"Blind as a tick for two weeks," Porter replied.

"Prohibition will sober him up."

"Lucky for him, we'll all be sober come July."

Ludlow picked me up by my armpits and led me to a table next to an open window.

"Decided to commit suicide," I said.

"When?"

"Tomorrow morning. Going to take a room at the Biltmore, get a hot bath, and open a vein."

"Don't be morbid. Why don't you get a good night's sleep and we'll talk it over in the morning," Ludlow said sensibly.

I gazed at Ludlow. I trusted him. "Did you ever get this way?"

"It's my chronic state."

"I can't go on. She's a once-in-a-lifetime blend," I said, while trying to climb through the window. It was on the second story, and I could have seriously hurt myself if I jumped out. Ludlow pulled me back into the club.

"That's enough for one day, old boy."

Back at my hideous apartment, I crooned, swaying up the stairs, brushing against the peeling walls.

Inside, I rushed into the bathroom and vomited.

Never confuse a single defeat with a final defeat.

Sunlight seemed to reflect off my pale skin as Ludlow and I ambled past a boarded-up bar that had "Prohibition" scrawled on the door.

"Are you certain about going back west?" he asked.

"There's nothing else left for me. The only thing to do now is to return to literature. It's my ace in the hole."

When we reached the Barron Collier Advertising Agency, Ludlow waited outside as I entered.

I avoided the stares of my co-workers as I made a beeline for Mr. Collier's office.

"Morning, Mr. Collier."

He took his glasses off. "Well, Mr. Fitzgerald, we haven't seen you in a couple weeks."

"No, sir. I'm quitting."

"I'm sorry. I believe you had the talent to make it in the advertising business," he said, sounding a little hurt.

"You believe in very little."

"You don't have to be nasty about it."

I nodded. "I apologize. You've been very kind."

"You'll be back."

I would not be back. I had literary success at a young age waiting for me. But it would not be the last time I pulled myself up from loss. Later, my losses manifested as poverty, alcoholism, and Zelda's schizophrenia.

In a real dark night of the soul it is always three o'clock in the morning, day after day.

V

AS I RODE BACK to St. Paul through the wide-open plains of the Midwest, I edited *The Romantic Egoist*. I paced up and down the train, talking to myself, acting out scenes in my mind. I enjoyed the other passengers observing me as if I were mad.

On my first night back, my father, mother, sister, and I sat in the dining room. The mood was restrained until my mother said, out of nowhere, "We all think it's fine you want to write a novel, dear, but wouldn't it be better if you worked and wrote at the same time? You're going to have to sooner or later. Writing really isn't a position."

My father came to my defense.

"Unless he turns out to be a Longfellow or Wordsworth."

"Well, that's different." My mother gaped at my father. "Of course, we'll support you in this endeavor, except financially. You know that we don't have it like we used to," my mother said, glancing at my father. "And it might be best for you not to have any spending money. It may distract you, and the sooner this is out of your system, the better."

"This will never leave my system. I don't have a choice."

"Of course you have a choice. God gave us all free will."

In the attic, I taped up my novel's plot on the wall above the desk. I sat back and flipped through the manuscript, slashing out lines, writing in margins. I rarely left the house for months.

"It's unnatural—a boy locked in his room all day and night. He claims he's enjoying himself," my mother repeated various times.

"I imagine he is," my father would say, before or after sneaking a drink from his flask.

Each morning, I began writing at seven o'clock on a fresh piece of paper. I would sit for hours just streaming the possibilities through my mind before inspiration snatched me up for that day's writing.

To clear my head, I went out for walks on the crisp, cold evenings. The red-hot tip of my cigarette would warm my face as my footsteps scratched against the pavement.

One evening, a bright light blinded me on the side of the road. I squinted away when I recognized Reuben Warner's chuckle.

Reuben balanced himself on top of the front seat of his sparkling green Stutz Bearcat. Tubby sat in the passenger's side. Reuben slid his hand across the side of his new car.

"Pretty slick, huh?"

I whistled my approval.

"Sure is," Tubby said.

"Not only that, I have something you can't find anywhere in St. Paul these days. Scott, you're going to appreciate this." Reuben reached down and pulled up an unlabeled bottle. "Bathtub gin, the best in the West."

"Where did you find that?"

"Connections, Scott. Connections. Hop in and we'll sample this rare vintage."

"Hop in, Fitz," Tubby agreed.

Tubby and Reuben slid over.

"Aren't you coming, Scott?" Tubby asked.

I retreated. "I can't. Thanks. I have a schedule to keep."

"Schedule? Whattaya mean, schedule? You don't have a job," Reuben said.

"Come on, Fitz. One night. You've barely been out since you've been back," Tubby said.

"When I'm finished. I promise." I hurried away from the temptation, down the dark street.

"I'm glad I'm not a literary man," I heard Reuben say.

At home, my mother and father were drinking tea with a respectably tailored man named Mr. Cooper.

"It's not often that opportunity knocks at a young man's door," Mr. Cooper said.

"So true," my mother agreed.

My father's expression seemed distant.

"Scott, this is Mr. Cooper, of Briggs-Cooper Advertising," my mother said.

Mr. Cooper eagerly shook my hand. "The largest advertising firm in St. Paul."

"It's nice to meet you," I said, attempting to gracefully fade away upstairs.

"Scott, you don't understand," my mother spoke through her clenched smile. "Mr. Cooper is here to see you." She patted the chair where she wanted me to sit.

I sat.

"Father Joe told me you were a very creative and energetic young man with a fine education," Mr. Cooper hesitated, but I remained mute. "Scott, I know you have experience with a large New York agency, but what I'm interested in is investing in your youth. I want someone in touch with the changing times. That's why I'd like you to be the advertising director in my firm. At a very generous starting salary, I may add."

Mr. Cooper's offer should have been a tempting one. I was broke and privately unsure that my writing would make a dime.

My mother sighed with happiness. Mr. Cooper, proud of what he offered, waited for my gratitude.

"You are making a grave mistake—I am not your man. I have neither energy nor creativity for advertising. I'm sorry, but I have work to do."

I believe I caught my father smile.

"Scott, think about what you're saying. You don't receive offers like this every day. This is an excellent opportunity," my mother said.

My mother searched for help from my father. She didn't get it.

"It's his free will," my father said.

My mother must have turned to the stunned Mr. Cooper. "More tea, Mr. Cooper?" she asked.

After a three-hour writing session, I lay on my bed, staring at the ceiling, exhausted. Rolling over onto my side, I was barely able to keep my eyes open. I glanced at a photo of Zelda and drifted off.

I woke when the photograph slid to the floor. I picked it up and propped it up on my desk and continued to write.

Later that week my mother set up an appointment for me to speak with the parish priest, Father Joe Barron.

"I love the new title, Father—*This Side of Paradise.* It's from a Rupert Brooke poem. Poetic, isn't it?"

Father Joe seemed a little preoccupied as we strolled around the rectory. "Yes, very nice. Very poetic. All that's extraordinary. A young man who is so talented, but to turn down the Briggs-Cooper position? Do you think that was wise? It's good to have something to fall back on. You wouldn't have to be there forever."

"I can't imagine doing anything like that ever again."

Father Joe and I stopped in front of the rectory.

"It's more than that. I've noticed you're rarely at mass since you have been back."

"Religion and literature don't seem to have much to do with each other."

"Scott, don't be a damned fool. You can be a practicing

Catholic and a popular writer, too. I know there aren't many at the moment. You could change all that."

Father Joe made sense, but I felt only alienation and rebellion toward the Church. "Maybe it's only my youth, but Catholicism is scarcely more than a memory."

"What are you going to do if the novel doesn't sell?"

"I haven't considered that."

"You're only sending it to one publisher. What are the chances? One in a hundred? One in a thousand?"

"They've already shown keen interest."

"I'm not trying to squash your dreams. Just have a backup. I know that's what your parents want as well," Father Joe pleaded.

"I know what I need, Father."

For a moment, I caught a glimpse into my unshakable faith that I was destined to be a great writer. Father Joe didn't realize it, but he had exposed that faith to a new vulnerability, and for a fleeting second I wanted to throw myself on the ground and admit I had doubts.

After I mailed off my manuscript, I lay on my bed for many weeks, just staring at the ceiling. Sometimes I sat outside my parents' house, waiting for the postman. My mother found me a job at the railroad and I tried to work. I was terminated because I preferred to sit down while hammering. I did see Tubby, but I had no money and all sorts of little debts. I lost eleven pounds.

One day, Reuben Warner came rolling by in his Stutz Bearcat. "Well, if it isn't Shakespeare. Have you heard anything about your book?"

"Not yet."

"I'm going to the dance at the club. Why don't you come with me? It will be like old times."

"Maybe I'll meet you there later," I lied.

"Good luck with the book, old sport."

I went by the club, but I only stood outside, looking in at friends enjoying a fun night out.

The next day, facing the window, I tapped a pencil against the arm of my chair. I rose and investigated a pack of cigarettes on my desk, only to discover that there were no more left. I returned to the window and noticed the mailman, who was unusually late.

Buttoning up my shirt, I jogged down the stairs.

My mother, humming something happily, was sorting through the mail.

"Mother, is there any mail for me?"

"I don't think so—bill, bill, bill. Oh, here you are, dear."

Without paying much attention, she handed me my letter from Scribner and walked out. I neatly opened it. I closed my eyes and screamed before I raced into the sitting room and kissed my startled mother.

"I've done it! Scribner accepted. I've done it."

My father entered.

I embraced him and almost cried.

"Congratulations, son," he said, with what appeared to be a mixture of regret, excitement, and pride.

My mother looked up to heaven and crossed herself.

"I did it."

I ran out of the house and down the street. I caught up with the mailman and hugged him.

"Hey!" he yelled.

"Thank you—you've saved my life."

Before the mailman could ask how, I ran off.

I ran down the middle of the road toward a car, forcing it to a full stop. Inside the car, a placid man and woman gaped at my unrestrained joy.

"My novel is going to be published!"

"That's very nice," the man said.

"Congratulations," the woman offered.

I considered the couple's frozen smiles and then ran off.

I had my hair cut and my shoes shined, and later enjoyed a victory cigar and some bathtub gin with Reuben and Tubby.

Before Reuben dropped us off, we shook hands, displaying our deep respect and affection for one another, despite our long rivalry. Tubby and I hopped out.

"I'm happy for you, Scott. You deserve it," Reuben said.

Reuben zoomed off. Tubby and I hugged.

"Wish me luck," I said, crossing my fingers.

"You'll win her again."

I immediately began making plans to catch the next train to

New York to speak with Maxwell Perkins before I ventured down to Montgomery to see Zelda.

Everybody's youth is a dream, a form of chemical madness.

VI

INSIDE THE RED-BRICKED WORLD of Scribner, an efficient secretary opened the door and announced, "F. Scott Fitzgerald is here to see you, Mr. Perkins."

Maxwell Perkins came around the desk and grasped my hand. "It's good of you to come out. I can't tell you how happy I was to write you about the acceptance."

"I've been in a trance ever since I received your letter."

"The novel is so different that it is hard to prophesize, but Mr. Scribner and I are all for taking a chance and supporting it with vigor."

"With my friends at Princeton and in St. Paul, I'm sure it will sell at least twenty thousand copies minimum."

Max smiled as if he had heard this sort of boasting before. "If it sells five thousand, we will be extremely pleased."

I frowned and began to pace. "You wrote that it would be out in the spring?"

"Yes, late March."

"Would it be utterly impossible for you to publish the book

by Christmas? I have so much riding on its success—including, of course, a girl."

Max seemed to be taking me seriously. "You have to understand that first novels rarely make much money. To put your book out with no advance advertising—it would have no chance at all."

"Of course, you're right. It's probably too late to make a difference, anyway."

...the test of a first-rate intelligence is the ability to hold two opposed ideas in the mind at the same time, and still retain the ability to function. One should, for example, be able to see that things are hopeless and yet be determined to make them otherwise. This philosophy fitted on to my early adult life, when I saw the improbable, the implausible, often the 'impossible,' come true.

I didn't know what to expect, whether Zelda was married or had forgotten about me, but once again I stepped off the train in Montgomery. There were very few people in the station. I hesitated, and then started to walk. I turned around to see if she had appeared behind me. She had not, and I continued on alone.

On the cab ride to the Sayre house, I surveyed the familiar route. Montgomery seemed deserted in contrast to its energetic excitement during wartime.

"Do you remember me? Lieutenant Fitzgerald, 67th Infantry?" I asked the familiar driver.

"Sure. I remember you, Lieutenant."

I sat back; it was obvious by his manner and tone that he did not remember me.

Standing outside the Sayre house, I thought it seemed much smaller, more run-down.

Minnie answered the door and invited me into the library.

"Are you still working in New York, Scott?"

I was stunned anyone would suggest such a thing, that people didn't understand and see that my destiny was to become a brilliant writer. "No, no, I'm not. My novel is due out in March from Scribner."

"That sounds very nice."

"Zelda didn't tell you? I wrote to tell her."

"She never mentioned it. She should be down shortly, and you two can talk all about what you've been up to."

After Minnie exited, I waited for about ten minutes in the room full of memories. Zelda appeared, dressed casually.

"Hello, Scott."

"Hello."

"I haven't seen you for a long time."

"Over five months."

"How are you?"

"A little anxious for my book to come out."

"Congratulations."

"You'll recognize a character in it quite a bit like yourself."

"I'll have to read it."

"I don't know exactly what to say. Does it bother you, my being here?"

"No."

"Are you engaged?"

"No."

"Are you in love with anyone?"

"No."

"After all that's happened between us, I had to come back and see you."

Zelda's expression could have meant anything.

The room quickly became suffocating, and I suggested we go for a walk. Zelda agreed.

We strolled through the arched entrance of the Confederate Cemetery. She bent down near a grave and brushed the dirt from a flat headstone.

"Margery Lee, 1844-1867. She was only twenty-three when she died. I think perhaps a lot of men went away to war meaning to come back to her, but maybe none ever did; there's no record of marriage," Zelda said.

"Her name and date say it better than anything could."

"You see how it is, don't you?"

"You're beautiful, so I know she must have been."

We stared at each other, before Zelda rose and walked on through the white crosses that blanketed the graveyard.

"These are the saddest; they are all unknown," Zelda said.

She turned and stared at me. Everything seemed possible as we embraced.

My dreams came true. *This Side of Paradise* went to number one on the *New York Times* bestseller list the next year. Zelda and I were married in St. Patrick's Cathedral in New York City.

I died at the peak of my writing powers. Many believe *The Last Tycoon* would have been my finest novel. *The Great Gatsby* is considered among the greatest American fiction of all time.

And Zelda's fire still burns bright. Her painting and writing are now respected on their own merits. She was a woman ahead of her time, and she inspires women to pursue their dreams.

We opened the world for future generations, so we beat on... through the stories that we lived and created together.

Three A.M.

AFTER I EARNED A BA in comparative literature in my twenties, I traveled in Europe for two months with a blonde girl who reminded me of Zelda Fitzgerald. That is to say, she was a golden girl and a Leo. Astrology seemed to matter somewhat at the time.

When we returned, we were telling each other I love you. She found an apartment on Laurel Avenue in West Hollywood, and I moved in. I was broke, with no idea how to find work and with zero job skills. I only lasted a couple of hours at a telemarketing gig I was hired at in L.A.

This was after an amazing final semester with Professor Gervais, who made F. Scott Fitzgerald's writing and *The Great Gatsby* come to life with promise, romance, and youth. It was just after Europe and college that I started to read Fitzgerald's biography and was stunned to learn that I was staying on the same street he had lived on in his final year. He had died at Sheilah Graham's apartment a few blocks away, off Sunset Boulevard.

Then the idea popped into my head to write a screenplay about Scott and Zelda. No one had made a film about their early lives. I avoided thinking about their later failures and focused on their beautiful romance and Scott's huge early success.

I entitled it *Young Scott and Zelda*. This is not that story. This is the story of failure, disintegration, and waste.

When Scott and Zelda first moved to New York, Scott saw Zelda outside of her home state of Alabama for the first time. When he watched her walk confidently down the street, he realized she was wildly out of place, with her frills and furbelows, and this upset him because he was self-conscious about fitting in, about being one of the smart crowd, about being one of the upper classes. Those people understood what to wear in New York City.

He immediately enlisted his friend Marie Hersey to remake Zelda's style.

"You need to take my fiancée shopping. She can't go around New York looking like that."

Scott and Zelda, both fair and beautiful, stood at the altar of St. Patrick's Cathedral. Only Scott's Princeton pal Ludlow Fowler, Zelda's sisters Marjorie and Rosalind, and Rosalind's husband Newman Smith were in attendance.

Neither Scott nor Zelda were religious. This isn't unusual for those in their teens and twenties in any age. Priests and bishops tried to recruit Scott to be a Catholic writer. But Scott saw Catholicism as a renunciation of life and living well. His short story "Absolution" contains a sentence that reveals Scott's view: "There was something ineffably gorgeous somewhere that had nothing to do with God."

You never get the sense that Zelda was a believer at all as she grew up. And neither of them seemed to treasure those aspects of spirituality—such as charity, thriftiness, wisdom, and humility—that could have guided them throughout their lives.

It is ironic that the priest at their wedding sent them off with these words: "Zelda, you be a good Episcopalian, and Scott, you be a good Catholic, and you'll get along fine."

They rode on the roofs of taxis, drank champagne, and became the toast of Manhattan in 1920. They wanted to have fun and expected to be the center of attention. They were bursting with life and rejoiced in jolting anyone from the mundane or routine.

Once, in a taxi, Scott cried out, "I know I'll never be this happy again." I believe this turned out to be true.

Scott wanted to be a successful artist with money in the city with Zelda. A reasonable goal for someone in his early twenties, and he was the one in a million who accomplished it. His goal never really changed as his youthful success receded further from him as each year passed. Fitzgerald's well-documented decline was buffered by his stubbornness and refusal to pivot or change when things went wrong. Zelda, too, had that blindness that never allowed her to try to build or demand a stable life.

Their downfall would have been less likely today. Scott would have had resources to help him quit drinking, and Zelda would have had options as a woman to start her own life and career. I'm pretty sure she would have left Scott if their story had taken place sixty years in the future.

With their arms locked, they skipped down Fifty-Seventh Street. They were the media's poster children for the Roaring Twenties.

Their early relationship was also filled with an innocent tenderness, reflected in their letters to each other.

"Let us never spend a night apart," Scott said.

"Never," Zelda agreed.

"Nobody's got any right to live but us."

"They're dirtying up our world, and I can't let them because I want you so much."

"Even if you ran away with another woman and starved and beat me...I would still want you."

Scott's ability to write gorgeous sentences was based on a romantic nature. He was searching for someone to adore. Zelda was sunny and shiny and expected to be loved and to be the center of the universe.

Scott is not often compared to George Orwell. I think it's interesting to do so because they are such opposites, so this is the first of many contrasts I'll make between them. Orwell was not seduced by bright shiny things like Fitzgerald was. Orwell wanted to lift up the down-and-out and believed it his mission to help the poor and make their lives better.

Scott and Zelda were rock stars in their time. Their hotel suite in downtown New York was a mess: ashtrays, half-empty glasses, dishes, papers, books scattered about. In the room lounged handsome young men and women, including C. Lawton Campbell, Ludlow Fowler, John Peale Bishop, Marie Hersey, Anita Loos, Alexander McKaig, George Jean Nathan, and Townsend Martin.

Scott could have been a magazine model decked out in a new Brooks Brothers suit. Scott waved around a five-dollar bill that was on fire and lit his cigarette with it, and then tossed the burning bill into an ashtray.

While Zelda bathed, she shouted into the other room. "Scott, tell Lawton about last night. Scott, tell Lawton about the spinach and champagne. Did you tell Lawton about our fight?"

"Our marriage can't last. We're doomed," Scott said.

Zelda entered wearing only a fur coat.

And it's true they threw wild, Gatsby-style parties when they rented a house on Long Island. Flappers, writers, artists, theater people, cartoonists, Scott's college friends, and friends of friends of friends attended the festivities.

"Visitors are requested not to break down doors in search of liquor, even when authorized by the host or hostess," Scott and Zelda informed them.

Croquet was played on the lawn at night with car headlights illuminating the game.

"Weekend guests are respectfully notified that invitations to stay over until Monday issued by the host or hostess during the small hours of the morning must not be taken seriously."

Outside, someone drove his or her Model T into the water. A few attractive women waded out of the car as a crowd gathered to watch several men try to keep the vehicle from sinking.

Everything seemed innocent. However, Scott and Zelda's demons and immaturity began to create conflict between their two competing personalities.

When the beautiful actress Laurette Taylor arrived at his party, Scott ran to her. "My God, you beautiful egg. You beautiful egg."

Zelda retaliated by cuddling with George Jean Nathan and wrapping her arms around him.

Scott jealously watched George nibbling on Zelda's neck, so he escorted Laurette Taylor to the sofa where he fell to his knees and sat at her feet, while keeping his eye on Zelda.

Later, Rosalind and Zelda enjoyed cocktails at a table on the lawn. A drunk Scott approached them. He reached for a drink on the table, but he accidently snagged the tablecloth and yanked on it, crashing all the glasses and bottles onto the grass.

He weaved toward the water of Long Island Sound and then passed out beneath a tree.

When Scott woke up, the party had quieted down but there were still a few stragglers. He picked himself up and wandered into the house, discovering Zelda and Rosalind in the kitchen.

There were dirty dishes, bottles, and discarded food everywhere. He spotted a leg of lamb, then flung it at them.

"You're drunk," Rosalind said.

"Of course, I'm drunk. I'm an alcoholic."

"Go to bed," Zelda said.

"You necked with half the men here tonight. I'm going to kill you both."

Rosalind and Zelda attempted to escape, but Scott threatened them with a lit candelabrum. He heaved it at them, barely missing.

"You're insane!" Rosalind said.

"He's just an Irish cop like his father," Zelda said.

Scott slapped Zelda across the face.

"You coward," Zelda said.

"I'm sorry. I didn't mean to hit you. I'm sorry."

Zelda pulled away from him.

"Let's go, Zelda. I'll take you back to Montgomery. You can't live like this. Not with him." Rosalind held Zelda's arm.

"If Scott and I want to live in this manner, I will brook no interference from anyone," Zelda said.

They were a couple that remained together for better or worse, mostly for worse. Why? They could have married others. Zelda was a terrible wife for a writer; Scott was a terrible husband for someone like Zelda.

Perhaps it came from their relationships with their families. Scott's mother was eccentric, and she embarrassed him. He didn't even show up for her funeral. He imagined that his parents were other people and in reality, royalty. He admired his father's good manners, but his father had failed at business and was a quiet presence in a house that his mother dominated.

Zelda's father was a conservative right-wing judge. She respected and loved him, but there was an emotional disconnect between the two. And her mother doted on her. Zelda loved her mother, but I don't think she wanted to emulate her. Zelda yearned to be free.

A sign next to a pyramid of copies of Scott's first book, *This Side of Paradise*, in the Scribner's bookstore celebrated it as the best-selling book in the US. Zelda was watching the book party festivities, a little bored, when an *Esquire* writer approached her.

"Hi, Zelda. Arnold Gingrich, *Esquire* magazine."

Zelda stared down the street. "That is a male street, isn't it?"

Arnold peered down the street at linear structures and brownstones. He seemed a little confused for a beat.

"Would you mind if I ask you a few questions?"

Zelda brightened. "I don't mind."

"Did you like *This Side of Paradise*?"

"I adored it. Especially the parts plagiarized from my diary and letters."

Scott appeared by her side. "Zelda is the most charming person in the world. She's perfect."

The writer transcribed their conversation on a notepad.

"You don't think that. You think I'm a lazy woman."

"I think you're perfect. You're always ready to listen to my manuscript at any hour of the day and night. And you do, I believe, clean the icebox once a week."

"Are you ambitious, Zelda?" Arnold asked.

"Not especially. I want to be myself and enjoy living."

"What would you do if you had to earn your own living?"

"I've studied ballet. If I wasn't successful, I'd try to write."

Zelda, like many girls in their late teens, just wanted to have fun. She was always eager to go out, making Scott's life as a writer and husband difficult. That meant that he got up late and didn't write at all some days. She would say, "You're such a spoilsport and kill-joy." And she made him jealous by threatening to go where there would be an ample number of single men. Scott succumbed to these threats and went along.

Hemingway had driven an ambulance in Italy during World War I and Orwell was a policeman in Burma in the twenties. During this time, Fitzgerald was being led to clubs by his spoiled wife. In fact, he remained self-centered and didn't become involved in any causes. It's no wonder he crumbled. He could have been so much more than he was. He left the field to Hemingway, Camus, Steinbeck, Orwell, and others. He never wrote about the poor or seemed to care about them or politics or war in a serious way. His success came so early that he had no chance to discover himself or the world.

Scott and Zelda met with their gang, partying at an elaborate speakeasy, perhaps the Jungle Club.

What happened next was predictable.

"You've had enough," a husky bouncer said to Scott.

"Everyone in this establishment has had enough," Scott said.

"I've seen you in here before. We're cutting you off."

"Who are you to tell me anything? I'll inform you when I've had enough."

When Scott threatened to punch the bouncer in the face, Lawton stepped between them.

"Scott, old boy, I've been looking for you. I have a drink for you at my table."

Scott glared at the bouncer.

"I've been wanting to talk to you about your story in the *Post*," Lawton added.

Scott began to laugh as if this were funny. So did Lawton.

Lawton escorted Scott away from the bouncer and trouble.

"You read my short story?"

"Every word."

Zelda marched up to them. "Hey, why did you ditch me at the bar?"

"I saved you a seat, Zelda." Lawton gestured toward his table.

"I didn't ditch you," Scott said.

"I was waiting at the bar all by myself. You ditched me!"

"The bouncer refused to let me buy a drink with my hard-earned cash because he said I'd had enough."

Lawton scratched his head and appeared worried as he listened to Scott and Zelda bicker back and forth.

"Scott, you're not going to let them get away with that. If you want a drink, why shouldn't you have one?"

"I should be able to drink anytime I like."

"You've had enough," the bouncer said when Scott demanded to be served.

"Scott, you're not going to let him say that to you, are you?" Zelda asked.

"I've had enough of you." Scott's punch glanced off the bouncer. He wound up and swung wildly but missed. Scott was a better fighter than most people realized and could hold his own in a scuffle, though he lost his fair share because he would take on anyone, in any situation.

The bouncer shoved Scott halfway across the room, knocking down tables and chairs.

"Get up and fight like a man, Scott. Get up and show him," Zelda egged him on.

The next morning Scott lay in bed. His head was bandaged. One eye was almost closed and black.

Lawton came to see him. "How are you feeling?"

"What happened last night? I don't remember a blessed thing," Scott said.

Lawton ignored the opportunity to explain the previous evening. "Is Zelda okay?"

"Oh, she's fine. She's gone to exchange our tickets. We were sailing for Europe today."

It was at this time that Zelda became pregnant and had their only child, a girl, Scottie.

It's said that moments after giving birth, Zelda proclaimed, "Oh God, goofo. I'm drunk. Mark Twain. Isn't she smart."

Scottie hiccupped.

"She has the hiccups. I hope she's beautiful and a fool—a beautiful little fool."

Having a child did not appear to affect Scott and Zelda's lifestyles. Now there was another mouth to feed, so he had to keep selling out his talent for money. At the same time, he was writing *Gatsby*. That's something to always keep in mind with them. They created *Gatsby* together. Only a few novels compare to its combination of story, characters, mood, plot, and style. Hemingway and Gertrude Stein and many others knew it immediately. And, of course, it did not sell nearly as well as his previous two novels.

Gertrude Stein said this about Scott's writing: "*The Great Gatsby* will be remembered when your contemporaries are forgotten." This talk annoyed Hemingway, but he might have believed it to be true. It wasn't. Hemingway's books still sell well as do Fitzgerald's today.

Orwell wrote terrific prose, but he could never write a beautiful or poetic novel like *Gatsby* or *Tender is the Night*. It was a rare gift that Scott possessed. Hemingway said of Scott's talent: "His talent was as natural as the pattern that was made by the dust on a butterfly's wings. At one time he understood it no more than the butterfly did and he did not know when it was brushed or marred."

Zelda was a part of Scott and his writing. Scott, like many novelists, needed a backdrop, a connection to his world, and every one of his books metamorphosed into a story about Scott and Zelda. Zelda suffered from not having an outlet.

They moved to France like everyone else. This is where Scott met Hemingway, young, tall, handsome, and extremely confident. Scott was immediately infatuated with "Hem" and his writing.

"You're the new voice. If I didn't already have a style, I'm sure I'd emulate you," Scott said.

"You've written a fine novel now. And you mustn't write slop."

"I have to write stories that sell."

"Write the best story that you can and write it as straight as you can."

"I write the stories without compromising, then change them to make them commercial."

"Bullshit!"

"I need to sell them so I can write good books."

"You'd be the greatest writer in the world if you weren't married to Zelda."

Scott tucked his hands in his pockets.

"Loan me some money."

"Sure, Hem."

Did Hemingway really talk like that? I think he did on some level. And it's fun to write about him that way. These two men were connected, whether they liked it or not. Scott realized it immediately, but I don't think Hemingway did until later.

One of the legends of Scott and Zelda was that something out of the ordinary happened when they were around. They loved to put people on the spot. Even Hemingway was given this treatment when Scott pestered him with questions about whether he had slept with his first wife, Hadley, before they were married.

Zelda hated Hemingway, perhaps because he was someone who would not put up with her.

Here is a fictional example based on real quotes of Scott, Zelda, Ernest, and his charming wife, Hadley, socializing together.

Scott was in an ebullient mood. "Max believes *Sun* will be a sensation," he said, referring to Hemingway's new book, *The Sun Also Rises*, due to come out at Scribner's.

"It's all bullfighting, bull slinging, and bullshit," Zelda said.

"Zelda is just kidding. She's not serious," Scott said.

Zelda remained silent, but it was obvious she was not kidding.

Hemingway claimed in *A Moveable Feast* that Zelda leaned toward him and asked, "Do you think Al Jolson is greater than Christ?"

The story is probably true because she asked the same thing of others. Zelda was losing her mind and spirit. She was out of her element with no parents or family or friends or religion or job or anything to help support her. And she and Scott had constant money problems.

You get the feeling Hemingway was much more on Scott's mind than Scott was on Hemingway's. Hemingway was pumping out books, marrying, dating, fishing, hunting, and fighting, while Scott slowly slipped into despair and loss.

"He's a pain in the neck, talking about me and borrowing money from you while he does it," Zelda said.

"I won't take you criticizing Hem. He's beyond reproach," Scott said.

"He's as phony as a rubber check and you know it."

"You're just jealous."

"Of what? A pansy with hair on his chest?"

"If you say anything bad about him, you are crazy."

"He thinks I'm crazy and says so. Why shouldn't I say anything I choose about him?"

"You insulted the most talented young writer of our generation."

"I didn't insult him. I just said he was a phony."

"He's pure, unlike me, writing trash for the *Post*."

"I like your stories."

"They're a sellout. You just love the lifestyle they buy."

At a certain point in their marriage, it was all about hurting each other.

"You'll never be able to satisfy a woman," Zelda said to Scott.

"You've been awfully satisfied at times."

"I'm glad you think so."

Scott didn't want to argue with her and rolled out of bed.

"It's the way you're built."

"The way I'm built?"

"It's unsatisfactory."

"How do you know?"

"A woman knows."

"You're vicious. I'm going to work."

"Work? You mean drink."

When this conversation enters a relationship you know it's over, and you'll do anything to humiliate your partner. To be vicious was why Zelda said it.

Scott was ingenuous enough to bring Hemingway into his sexual problems with Zelda. Hemingway then exploited Scott's confidences, when he made the Fitzgeralds' most intimate issues public. It was his chance to humiliate Fitzgerald and sully his reputation. Perhaps he was motivated by jealousy or perhaps he wanted to needle Scott and Zelda, who were such pains in the ass.

"She's crazy." Hemingway downed his drink in one gulp.

"Do women like a man's penis large or small?"

Hemingway must have been annoyed. "Did she say your penis is too small?"

"She said I couldn't satisfy a woman."

"That's the oldest trick in the book, old man. She's attempting to destroy you."

"Why did she say that?"

Hemingway frowned. "Come on. Let me take a look at you."

"You're really first rate."

"Buy me a drink."

When Zelda became pregnant again, she had one request. "I want an abortion." I wonder what made her choose to do this? It was something she said she would never do. Perhaps it was the unstable, wandering, stressful life they led. Perhaps she was worried about her figure. Perhaps she just didn't want to have another child with Scott. Perhaps she didn't feel she was up for a nine-month pregnancy and a baby, or she knew she was losing her mind and wouldn't be able to handle more responsibility.

After the abortion, Scott brought lilies to her hospital room, where Zelda lay feverish in bed.

"The lilies are talking to me," Zelda said.

Scott handed them to her.

"I feel like a thunderbolt has hit my stomach."

"I'll take care of you."

Zelda grasped his hand.

"Always."

"I know you will."

The *Tender Is the Night* period was a long, beautiful, and dark time in the mythic and stunning South of France in the 1920s. Gerald and Sara Murphy were socialites and key figures that this world orbited. They often threw parties. On their guest list were the Valentinos, Picasso, John Dos Passos, and Isadora Duncan. Gerald was a dandy, slender, fit, an artist with long sideburns. Sara was beautiful, refined, and intelligent.

Scott labored more than eight years writing the sometimes-gorgeous *Tender Is the Night*. It's another book about Scott and Zelda, a sad and drawn-out tale that is devoid of any reality, a sort of self-indulgent fantasy where no real person could exist. Fitzgerald's subject matter continues to be the opposite of Orwell's. Orwell tramped among the poor and homeless, whom he brings to life in his writings. Fitzgerald's characters are beautiful and even refined, but hard to believe. Even the Murphys felt the two main characters, Dick and Nicole Diver, who were supposedly based on them, were more like Scott and Zelda than them. Rosemary Hoyt was Scott's fantasy rich girl. Hemingway wrote to him after he read *Tender is the Night* and said: "You, who can write better than anybody can, who are so lousy with talent that you have to—the hell with it."

The Murphys and everyone else were delighted when Hemingway appeared on the scene. He was someone not impressed by or drawn to the rich.

"Hemingway is a delightful fellow. Where did Scott discover him?" Gerald Murphy asked Zelda.

Zelda didn't respond.

"I thoroughly approve of him," Gerald said.

"He's the real thing," Sara added.

Zelda remained poised and silent. Another small humiliation for her.

Gerald and Sara left Zelda, but not without a tender gesture by Sara, who touched Zelda's shoulder.

Zelda smiled politely.

It was at this time that Zelda met the handsome French naval officer, Edouard Jozan. He was likened to a Greek god. He was tall, handsome, bronzed, and had a brilliant smile. Did they have an affair? No one knows. Zelda certainly seemed to have been smitten. Their romance may have been one-sided, judging by Jozan's remarks much later. He had no intention of running off with her. He only remembered her as a nice person he swam with.

Scott and Zelda, as usual, were having money problems. They had blown through gobs of cash with little to show for it. They never owned a home their entire lives. Scott could have purchased a place in New York and rented it out. Practical thoughts such as these never seemed to occur to him.

They stayed together through everything, and the worst, much worse, was yet to come. Perhaps they stayed together for Scottie, but I don't think so.

Scott went out carousing and drinking while Zelda spent evenings with Jozan. Jozan maintained a different code than Scott. He was not a neurotic writer. The simple things gave him the most pleasure in life—flying, swimming, honor, bravery, and enjoying a fine bottle of wine.

"That's a wonderful list," Zelda said.

"However, I do love adventure," replied Jozan. "I dream of smoking opium in Indochina."

Zelda laughed.

One day, Jozan and Zelda gazed down from the picturesque cliff sixty-five feet above the ocean.

"Perhaps I should go first."

"I've dived off cliffs since I was a little girl in Alabama."

"Alabama! That sounds exotic." Jozan smiled.

She perched on the edge and jumped past the rocks into the narrow funnel that led to the ocean below. She made a small splash as she sliced into the sea.

Zelda emerged and flipped her hair back.

"Marvelous."

Jozan set himself and soared downward, piercing the water close to Zelda.

The force and speed of his dive surprised her. She laughed with pleasure.

Jozan surfaced. "Wooo!"

"Shall we do it again?"

"Of course."

Meanwhile, the Fitzgerald's marriage continued to deteriorate. It's humorous that Zelda accused Scott and Hemingway of being lovers during this period.

"I'm not going to sit around while you sycophants worship that phony," Zelda said.

"Quit saying that, Zelda. It's slanderous."

"The way you talk about him, I wonder if there's something more going on between you two."

"What are you saying? Are you accusing us of being fairies?"

Zelda took no notice of Scott and walked away.

"You're crazy if you think Hem or I are fairies. He's right. You are crazy!"

Zelda left the room.

"You are the one with lesbian tendencies."

Zelda and Jozan went out dancing while Scott went out drinking. Jozan wore his white naval uniform, and Zelda, tan with a lovely figure, was the other half of a strikingly handsome couple.

Gerald and Sara had observed the flirtation from the beginning. Sara gave Gerald a glance, as if to ask if Zelda and Jozan were really having an affair.

Scott stumbled home drunk and made a ruckus, tossing off his clothes and bumping into furniture and walls.

"Damn it. Hell."

He fell into their bed. Zelda lay still, waiting for him to paw her. She shoved him off when he did.

Scott passed out, and at some point, he mumbled, "No more, baby," in a reference she suspected was meant for Hemingway.

It's ridiculous to think that these two men were having an affair. It shows how reality had been lost on Zelda.

On the beach the next day, Zelda soaked up the sun as Gerald raked the rocks and seaweed off the sand. Sara relaxed with her shoulders bare and a string of pearls around her neck. Kids played in the surf.

Jozan's plane approached them. Zelda popped up eagerly and trotted toward the ocean, waving her arms.

The plane buzzed low and tilted its wings.

With their marriage crumbling, Zelda told Scott she wanted a divorce because she had fallen in love with Jozan.

"What is our marriage, anyway? It's been nothing but a constant battle ever since I can remember," she stated.

Scott was not going to accept a divorce. He claimed later that he and Jozan fought a dual, but he told many different stories to Hemingway concerning the whole affair. All of them different, but Hemingway was never the most reliable source.

I'm not sure how Scott could lock Zelda in their villa and forbid her from seeing Jozan. He evidently did get somewhat physical with her. And he likely went looking for Jozan.

"You're not going to throw away everything we've meant to each other for a summer flirtation," Scott said.

The reality of living on the French Riviera may be idyllic, but not if you have financial troubles and a deteriorating marriage like the Fitzgerald's. Living the good life had an ominous interior. The Great Depression was just around the corner.

There is no evidence of a major confrontation between Scott and Jozan. Jozan had himself transferred or was due to ship out. Perhaps he told Scott he'd be leaving soon. Perhaps Scott told him to leave Zelda alone and Jozan assented, or declared that he had no interest in absconding with Scott's wife. It was just a pleasant dalliance for him. Perhaps Scott did challenge him to a dual, but he refused.

"He will never fight for you or care about you like I will," Scott told Zelda.

We actually don't know what Scott told Zelda, but she was disappointed. She felt she had lost something important.

Scott was sorry it had all happened. He knew it was partly his fault. Perhaps Scottie reminded them both that their actions would affect more than themselves. The tension must have been awful.

Scott could be bullying with Zelda and passive-aggressive. It's easy to pick on marriage dynamics and dysfunction, but their relationship had become toxic and Zelda had few defenses.

At a party at the Murphy's, Scott flirted with Isadora Duncan, the famous dancer, who stroked his hair. Her intentions were less than honorable.

Scott loved or pretended to adore Isadora's attention. Perhaps he encouraged it because he knew it affected Zelda?

Zelda refused to acknowledge the attention Scott received. That was her great defense—to show nothing or not give any feelings away.

When someone bothered Zelda, she would say under her breath, "I hope you die on the marble steps."

However, it was Zelda who threw herself elegantly down a marble staircase when Scott became enchanted with Isadora.

Scott's arrogance and insensitivity surfaced when an old Frenchwoman, selling warm nuts and candies off a tray, visited the Murphy's deck. Her treats were delicious and partygoers came out to buy a snack from her.

Scott shocked everyone by giving her tray a football kick, sending it and the contents flying.

The Frenchwoman was completely mortified. The guests were horrified as well.

Scott tried to laugh as if it were all just a joke.

"Scott, what in God's name can you be thinking? This isn't a Princeton fraternity party," Gerald Murphy scolded.

It must have been impossible to live with someone like that.

Gerald Murphy tried to make amends by paying the woman for the nuts and apologizing.

I'd like to think the woman refused the money and left with her head held high.

It was the 1930s and the Depression was biting hard. There was Hitler and the winds of another world war. Orwell and

Hemingway were fighting in and reporting on the Spanish Civil War. And Fitzgerald was kicking the tray of a poor Frenchwoman.

Sara Murphy appeared at her husband's side. "If it wasn't for Zelda...I couldn't take him alone."

"I'm not sure I can take him, period. I'm banning him from our villa."

Everyone returned to normal, and they forgot about Scott. He hadn't forgotten about them.

He came around the house to some French doors, where he stood on the outside looking in, like a petulant little boy. He saw Zelda smile when Gerald poured her a glass of champagne.

Scott became enraged and grabbed a nearby trash can and flung it against the doors.

The noise startled everyone, but they realized it was Scott and returned to their drinks and conversations, further isolating him.

Diving home from the Murphy's there was an awful silence in the car as Scott drove Zelda home. When he stopped for an approaching train, Zelda's expression became peculiar. She let out an odd laugh. The rumble of gears and steel amplified her nervousness.

It chugged toward them, becoming louder and closer. Zelda wrung her hands as her eyes darted along the horizon. She jumped out of the car.

"Where are you going?"

Zelda ran toward the tracks.

"Zelda?"

Scott raced toward her, but it was a short distance between her and the rails.

"Zelda!"

Scott caught her and gripped her arm, propelling her around. She twisted back, attempting to pull away and leap in front of the train.

"What are you thinking? What's happening to you?"

He refused to let go and hugged her to the ground.

Zelda fought, but she had little strength. The heavy darkness flashed by, causing a surge of pressure that blew Scott's hair back. Out of breath, Scott fixed his eyes on Zelda, who was suddenly catatonic.

They returned to Paris and rented a depressing, dank apartment. Scott finished a glass of gin as he listened on the phone. He watched Zelda in the next room practicing ballet exercises, attitudes, and arabesques.

"Please trust me for a couple more weeks. Yes, of course. Thank you."

Scott hung up and entered where Zelda trained.

"Take some rest. You're overdoing it, dammit. In Russia they start at seven and you're nearly thirty."

"I don't need to rest. Dancing for Madame gives me the greatest joy."

Zelda had started training with renowned ballet teacher Madame Egorova.

Later, Scott peeked into the room at Zelda spinning into pirouettes. He was annoyed, worried, and baffled by her obsession.

And it was an obsession. Zelda threw her entire soul into ballet with the goal of being a prima ballerina. It was never going to happen. And at some point, Scottie had grown closer to Scott and simultaneously alienated from Zelda. And the dancing mania whirled Zelda into exhaustion.

Scott rubbed it in by declaring that she would never be a first-rate artist. Never.

Scott with a bottle of gin peered out the window as Zelda hurried from their dreary building to jump into a cab to go to class.

Zelda's cab became stuck in a traffic jam.

"I mustn't be late to dance for Madame. I mustn't be late, you see. Madame is expecting me."

The driver gestured at the traffic jam.

Zelda hopped out of the cab and began to run in her ballet slippers, absolutely panicked to make it to her lesson.

Zelda entered the studio and fell at the feet of Madame Egorova.

"I'm devoted to you, Madame."

"Please, Zelda, go prepare."

"Yes, Madame."

Scott continued to go out carousing and drinking. In the middle of the night, someone pounded repeatedly on the apartment door.

Zelda answered it. A taxi driver had to prop Scott up.

"Monsieur Fitzgerald," the driver said.

"Oh Scott, you said you wouldn't."

Scott staggered in. He snatched a figurine and smashed it on the ground, and then glared at Zelda.

"He did that because he knows that it is my favorite."

The taxi driver remained, wanting to be paid.

Scott woke with a terrible hangover but pulled himself together and rose. He heard Zelda practicing and glimpsed in.

She was incredibly thin. She appeared frazzled. Scott went back to bed.

When Scott woke again, he realized that it was silent in the apartment. He rose to find Zelda gazing out the window with a curious expression.

"What are you looking at?"

"I see odd things—people's arms too long or faces as if they were stuffed."

Scott followed her gaze. It was a normal day with regular people coming and going.

"One day the world between me and the others stopped. I was dragged like a magnet. I had headaches, and I could jump higher than ever." Zelda turned to a startled Scott. "I see humanity as a bottle of ants. Don't you?"

He couldn't breathe. "No."

"You forced me here...in a situation...feeling the vibrations of everyone I meet. Broken down."

He poured a drink at his desk in the other room and turned in Zelda's direction as if he could see through the wall. He began to panic, splashing gin outside his glass.

This was the end result for her. She was now a tragic figure. Was it Scott's fault? Her fault? What about the history of mental illness in the Sayre family? Zelda's brother Anthony was diagnosed with manic depression and committed suicide by jumping out of a hospital window. Zelda's sister Marjorie suffered a mental breakdown. So even if Zelda had remained in Alabama there was no guarantee she would have been mentally stable.

An unstable environment with money worries and constant change, an alcoholic husband, abortions, all had to factor into her downfall.

The easy answer is: all of the above.

Scott took Zelda to a doctor, who recommended she find treatment at a mental hospital. The grounds resembled a splendid resort: groomed trees, sculptured hedges, and villas.

A frail Zelda wandered in the garden. Scott and the tall and aristocratic Dr. Oscar Forel strolled at a distance behind her.

"Schizophrenia? Are you certain she's not just exhausted

from this dancing obsession of hers?" Scott asked.

"We believe so."

"Is that curable?"

"In one in four cases, the patient completely recovers. Two in four make partial recoveries and remain delicate and slightly eccentric."

"And the fourth goes completely mad."

"To put it bluntly, yes."

Their lives resembled the emotional state and health of the United States. The Southern belle, the Irish kid from St. Paul. They met in the most unlikely of circumstances, their country at war. They roared in the twenties. Now it was payback time in the thirties: their Great Depression. And no one fell further than they did. It wasn't just money that deserted them. An emotional and psychic hollowness due to sin, pride, and lack of character enveloped them.

"She'll claim it's my fault she's here."

Dr. Forel considered this for a moment. "No one can cause someone to become schizophrenic."

This seemed to calm Scott.

"But your actions and lifestyle aggravated and accelerated the condition. It would help her and you a great deal if you quit drinking."

"My drinking is none of your business and has no bearing on her condition."

Dr. Forel frowned. "I consider this a dual case."

"I do not. I have to work."

Zelda sat on a bench. When Dr. Forel and Scott caught up, Scott sat alongside her and smiled.

"Lovely, isn't it? I think you'll be happy here until you feel better."

"My life has been so miserable that I'd rather be in an asylum than with you. Does that mean a thing to you?" Zelda asked.

"It does not mean a blessed thing."

"I'm sick of being beaten down or bullied into accepting your ideas about everything."

"I'm the one who deserves to be bitter. You've jeopardized my career and finances."

Dr. Forel had seen enough. "Scott, why don't you wait for me in my office?"

Scott leaned back defiantly.

"Please."

Scott accepted this, considering the situation. He turned to Zelda. "I'll come to see you every day."

Zelda reached out, and they grasped hands for a moment, before an overwrought Scott hurried away.

"I'm so sick of compromise. Shearing off one part of myself after another until nothing's left," Zelda said.

"You won't have to compromise here," Dr. Forel said. "I'll have Scott keep his distance for a while."

"It doesn't matter. I don't get on with my husband, and I can't live without him."

The doctor and Scott thought it was a good idea for Scott to visit the ballet studio to get an appraisal of Zelda's talent. When he arrived, ballet lessons were in progress. Madame Egorova saw him and made her way over.

"How is Zelda?"

"Fine. She needs rest."

"Take a break. Dancers. Break."

"I'd like you to be completely honest concerning Zelda's ballet ability."

"She's a talented dancer."

"Is she a first-rate dancer, a prima ballerina?"

"No, she started too late for that. She could dance in the Follies or a supporting role in a company."

At the hospital, Zelda began her insulin shock therapy treatments. Three members of the staff pinned her down as Dr. Forel observed her. Zelda fought and struggled but the nurses strapped her arms. One tried to insert a guard between Zelda's teeth so she wouldn't bite her tongue. Zelda refused to open but the nurse forced the mouthpiece in.

Dr. Forel injected Zelda with insulin. Zelda's body went into immediate involuntarily seizure. After sixty seconds, she lay motionless.

Scott, Zelda, and Dr. Forel met in a bare room to give her the news about her ballet ability.

"I am not sick. I do not want to be hospitalized. I was brought here under duress. I wanted to return to dancing. Now I don't know what to do."

Scott and Dr. Forel exchanged glances.

"I'm devastated," Zelda said.

"I'm sorry, Zelda. We only inquired for your own good."

"What's to become of me? I have to work, but I can't anymore."

"Your ambition, inflated ambition, is one of the reasons for your breakdown. You've exhausted yourself from the dancing and competing with your husband. It's important that we reeducate you so you can be a good wife," Dr. Forel said.

"I don't need reeducating. Ballet was compensation for a miserable marriage."

After several months, Zelda was released, and Scott escorted her out of the hospital. He guided her in a tender and gentle manner. Zelda appeared healthy and rested, a smile on her face.

"Let's go home," he said.

Where was home? They never stayed in one place long. I grew up in a small town on the Central Coast of California and lived in Santa Barbara as well. I spent a couple of years in San Francisco, three years in San Diego, and over six years in the Los Angeles area. I understand Scott and Zelda's rootlessness. If they could have found a home, maybe none of this would have happened. Neither was at home with themselves.

They decided to live in North Carolina. They rented a house, where they sat at a large, long table for meals. There was little conversation. They avoided looking at each other.

When Zelda finished eating, she dropped her napkin and fork on her plate and walked off without a word.

Scott displayed no emotion and continued to pick at his food.

In a large upstairs room with an ancient, unused fireplace, Zelda started a novel that became *Save Me the Waltz*. When Scott entered, she ignored him.

"I told you if I came in and found you writing, I would crumple it up," Scott said.

"I do not want you to tear it up. You know that some of it is awfully good prose, and you know it would break my heart to tear it up."

"You know I would not do it."

"You reek of alcohol." She didn't allow him to argue. "Well, it's the truth...it is one of the reasons why I wanted to write, because you're drunk all the time, and I have nothing to do."

"That is my material. None of it's your material."

"Your material! You've taken my diaries, my words, my life, and put them into your novels. Now the asylums, the madness, the terrors are your material? Funny, I hadn't noticed."

"Everything we do is mine."

Zelda bit her lip and massaged the terrible skin rash on her neck.

"Think of our interests. It didn't matter that you wanted to be a third-rate ballet dancer, but if you want to be a third-rate writer, it hurts us. I am a professional novelist, and I am supporting you."

This was a low blow, and Zelda's acrid expression reflected the sting. "I want to be independent from you in every way. When you say something that is not so, then I want to do something so good that I can say 'That is a damn lie' and have something to back it up," she said.

"I won't let Max publish anything before I go through it and take out what's mine," he said before leaving.

With Scott gone, Zelda ripped off her clothes and flung them into the fireplace. She struck a match and lit it. She watched them burn. However, this fireplace had not been used in years and was plugged up. Smoke started to fill the room. Zelda didn't seem to care.

Firemen doused the flames on the second floor. A fireman came out of the house, sweating and coughing. Scott appeared, eager to please, with a tray of lemonade. He went to the firemen and served each a glass. They appreciated it.

Scott offered the grateful fire chief a refreshment.

"Any idea how the fire started?" the fire chief asked.

"I suspect the faulty wiring on the second floor," Scott said.

The fire chief nodded as if that were plausible.

Zelda watched in the distance.

Tender Is the Night was published to decent reviews. However, no one cared about rich people living in the South of France in the middle of the Depression. It horrified Zelda when she read it.

"God damn you! God damn you. God damn you."

"Dear, what's wrong? Are you all right?" Scott asked.

"You used me. You used my letters from the hospital, my treatments...you used everything I've been through."

Scott eventually needed to face the Sayres—Rosalind, Judge Sayre, and Zelda's mother, Minnie.

Zelda had relapsed, and the doctors had recommended that she be admitted to Highland Hospital.

"She doesn't need a hospital. She needs to come home and rest, that's all," Minnie said.

"You're to blame. Your drinking and lifestyle and cruelty," Rosalind said.

"You're not good for my daughter; you're too selfish. What you want always came first," Minnie said.

"The doctors stated that our lifestyles may have accelerated this, but no more than you raising her selfish, spoiled, and dependent."

"You're a liar. You crippled her," Rosalind said.

"You misled the doctors and me concerning the history of mental illness in your family," Scott said.

Minnie began to cry.

"How dare you, Scott! How dare you bring up our family tragedies," Rosalind said.

"It's important to tell the truth about her condition. Someone has to take responsibility. Minnie is an old woman and you are irreparably prejudiced against me." Scott knelt where Judge

Sayre sat. "You believe in me, Mr. Sayre. Please say you believe in me. I beg you to say that you believe in me. I love Zelda as much as you do. You know that's true."

"I believe you will always pay your bills, Scott," Judge Sayre said.

There were beer cans everywhere; Scott was drinking about forty beers a day. He chain-smoked. He sat around in a robe torn at the sleeves. No longer the pretty boy of his youth, he had developed a paunch. His hair was thinning. And tiny cracks appeared in his skin.

He dug through the rubble and mess searching for change. He counted a handful of coins.

On the stove were beans that he heated up. He ate them right out of the can.

Scott was broke and estranged from his family. His wife was in an asylum. His agent, Harold Ober, was raising his daughter. His books did not sell. He was an alcoholic. What does a man do at this point? Perhaps turn to God? Oscar Wilde did and wrote of his conversion beautifully in *De Profundis*. Scott remained consistent. He never changed. He had been humbled, but it never diminished his pride.

A lifeline came to Scott from Hollywood: writing screenplays. He desperately needed the money.

And it was at a party of writers, actors, producers, and film industry people where, in 1938, appearing antiquated in a salt-

and-pepper suit, he first laid eyes on the attractive gossip colum-
nist, Sheilah Graham.

Sheilah bore a striking resemblance to Zelda in his imagination.

"I like you," he told her.

"I like you, too."

"How old are you?"

"Twenty-seven. How old are you?"

"Forty." He grimaced.

"Of course, I've heard of you."

"What have you read?"

"I feel badly, I've actually never read any of your books."

"We'll have to do something about that."

"I want to read every one."

The following week, Scott and Sheilah explored a Hollywood
bookstore to find his books. The radio was on and they heard:
Sieg Heil! Sieg Heil! Sieg Heil! Sieg Heil! Sieg Heil!

"They're going to have another war—and we'll be in it, too,"
Scott said.

"It's terrifying."

"I'd fly over there and assassinate Hitler before he starts it. I'd
do it too, by God."

Sheilah held his arm.

"I wanted to fight in the last war, but they signed the armistice, and I never got over."

A middle-aged bookseller appeared.

"Good morning. Have you any books by Mr. F. Scott Fitzgerald?"

"Sorry, none in stock."

"Do you have any calls for them?"

"Oh, once in a while. But not for some time."

Sheilah held Scott's arm. "Let's try another bookstore?"

"To be out of print after having given so much. Even now there is little published in American fiction that doesn't bear my stamp in some small way. I was an original."

"I know another place we can try. I want to read this American original."

This, of course, was true. Scott was an original.

Gatsby has long been considered one of the greatest American novels ever. One other thing that was genuine was that he gave his entire life to creating fiction. I wonder how many people have committed themselves to their craft, but never made it and are now forgotten.

T.S. Eliot wrote that *The Great Gatsby* was the "first step forward in American literature since Henry James."

At Sheilah's apartment, Scott scanned photos of her sister, brother, grandfather, father, and mother.

"My mother died at seventeen. My rich aunt presented me at court. I found society boring, so I tried the stage, which led to New York, and I wrote an article that brought me to Hollywood."

"Where did your people come from? Is Graham Scottish? German?"

"Scottish." Sheilah's darting eyes betrayed nervousness in answering this question.

Scott suspected she was just sensitive about talking about her wealth.

"What was your father's name?"

Sheilah hesitated. "John Lawrence Graham."

"What was your mother's?"

"Veronica Roslyn Graham."

"What was your father's line of business?"

She stuttered. "He inherited money. He owned property."

"Where is your sister now?"

Sheilah turned away from him. "London."

"What school did you attend?"

Sheilah burst into tears.

"What is it? What is it?"

Scott sat alongside Sheilah on the sofa.

"What have I said to hurt you? I'm sorry, Sheilah. I had no idea—is there something you don't want to tell me? You needn't."

"If you must know, I never went to a real school, I was brought up in an orphanage. I left school when I was fourteen. I come from the slums of London, from the poorest, shabbiest people."

Scott slipped out his handkerchief and wiped her eyes. "Don't cry. I'm always so curious about everybody."

"I've lied and pretended. I'm phony. Oh, Scott, you'll hate me—my name's not Sheilah Graham, it's Lily Sheil. I'm not what you think at all."

"I wish I had known you then. I would have taken care of you."

"That's kind of you to say."

"I saw something in you last week that I haven't seen in twenty years."

"What was that?"

"My poor dead wife who is not dead, just in an asylum."

"Oh…"

Why did Scott fall in love with Sheilah? Was she half a person, sort of like Zelda was only half a person? Zelda grew up protected and spoiled and never worked a day in her life. Sheilah grew up poor and unprotected and had to work for everything she had. He only fell in love with someone with a giant vulnerability in her personality and history.

Scott and Sheilah attended Hemingway's showing of the Spanish Civil War documentary *Spanish Earth* to the film community. A who's who in Hollywood was at the event. Irving Thalberg, Norma Shearer, and Lillian Hellman were present.

Scott and Sheilah hid in the back. Everyone else crowded as close as possible to Hemingway.

"*Before, death came when you were old and sick. But now it comes to all in this village. High in the sky and shining silver, it comes to all who have no place to run, no place to hide.*" Hemingway punctuated the quote from the film by slamming a glass into a fireplace. The audience rose and applauded.

"If the Fascists take Spain, they won't stop there. Don't let the

Loyalists down. Show them that you support their righteous cause against the Franco fascist coup," Hemingway demanded.

The Hollywood community applauded again. They pulled out checks and cash that they dropped into a hat that was being passed around.

"Let's go," Scott said.

"Don't you want to talk to Ernest?"

"Not like this."

Sheilah nodded. "I understand."

"Let's sneak out before he sees me."

Scott believed Hemingway was as nervously broken down as he was, but it manifested itself in a different way. Hemingway's inclination was toward megalomania and Scott's was toward melancholy.

Scott had made several emotional, disastrous trips to see Zelda. This time she just stared out the window as if he weren't there.

"Zelda, won't you talk to me?"

Silence.

"Zelda, think about the impression you're making on the doctor."

Silence.

"I have a job in Hollywood. So you and Scottie don't have anything to be concerned about. There won't be anything to worry about financially. I just want you to get well."

Silence. A new doctor, Dr. Pine, appeared in the doorway.

Scott was overcome with sorrow, and he left the room with the doctor.

"My wife is a case, not a person."

"I do not believe she is schizophrenic."

"I never believed she was."

"But she hasn't responded to any of the treatments or to anyone."

"Our marriage is over. Still, it was a once-in-a-lifetime love."

Scott returned to Hollywood on the next flight. He became so inebriated he swayed down the aisle to his seat. He noticed a young woman. He smiled. "Isn't she pretty? Such lovely hair. Such poise."

The young woman blushed.

"You silly bitch."

The girl began to cry. Scott's nastiness wasn't lost on the other passengers and several arguments began.

A young man from the studio who knew Scott guided him to his seat.

"I read *The Great Gatsby*. The prose is brilliant, really, Mr. Fitzgerald. I'm in awe of your talent."

Scott gulped a drink from a flask. He burped.

"You ever mention that book again, and I'll slug you."

When he landed in Los Angeles, he bought a new bottle and gave the cab driver Sheilah's address. When they arrived, the cabbie was eager to get Scott out of his cab.

"Where do you live? Here?" He pointed to Sheilah's charming apartment in West Hollywood. "Help me out here, pal?"

"I'll help you out...by beating the holy crap out of you."

The cabbie threw up his hands as if he'd had enough.

A light came on in an apartment building. Sheilah jogged out.

"Here's my paramour, coming to rescue me."

Sheilah absorbed the verbal blow as she helped Scott into the house.

"You're drunk. I hate you when you're drunk."

Scott began to hop around and chant.

"Lily Sheil hates me when I'm drunk! Lily Sheil! Lily Sheil! She's a fake. Right out of the slums of London. Lily Sheil! Lily Sheil!"

Sheilah started to cry. Scott disappeared into a room and returned with a gun.

"You deserve better. I lost my life and wife so long ago. I'll make amends to you and my poor, sick wife by killing myself."

"Give me that gun. You're not killing yourself in my place."

Sheilah and Scott struggled for the gun. Sheilah got her hand on it, but Scott, even though drunk, had gone wild. He pushed her down and pointed the gun to his head.

"Shoot yourself, you son of a bitch. I didn't raise myself from the gutter to waste my life on a drunk like you," Sheilah said.

Scott lowered the gun.

"Get out! Get out!"

The Sayres eventually convinced Zelda to leave the hospital and come home. The doctor emphasized that if there was any sign of a relapse, they should bring her back to the hospital as soon as possible.

"She just needs to come home, and she'll be fine," Minnie said.

A nurse escorted Zelda to Minnie. It must have been a humiliating homecoming.

Back in Alabama, Zelda's shoes clicked on the sidewalk as she walked in her neighborhood. She wore clothes from head to toe, like an old spinster woman. She carried a Bible.

She passed a couple of children playing in their front yard. They pleased her.

"Hello, children."

"Hello."

"She's the crazy lady," the little boy whispered.

Zelda heard him. The children giggled.

When Scott sobered up, he was ashamed of himself. He tried for months to reach Sheilah, but she rejected any overture on his part.

She relented when he appeared at her door with a bouquet of flowers, hoping to see her one time at least.

"Sheilah, please. I want to apologize."

"You've already apologized."

"In person. Please, then I'll leave Hollywood and you alone forever if that's what you like. I beg you to hear me out just once."

Sheilah unlocked the deadbolt.

Sheilah positioned herself straight and proper on the sofa. Scott sat at the edge of a chair.

"I feel I'm partly responsible for what happened to Zelda. Before I met you, it was three o'clock in the morning for me no matter what time it was or where I was."

Sheilah displayed no outward reaction.

"I started to drink because everyone else drank and I enjoyed it. Then I needed liquor to write. And then I found I needed liquor just to get up in the morning."

"You are a different person when you drink."

"When I drink, I'm unfit for human association. I'm done. I haven't had a drop in two months."

"Don't alcoholics always say that?"

"I've hurt you deeply, I know. And if you want me to, I'll leave Hollywood and your life forever. I love you, Sheilah. If you give me one more chance, I promise you, I'll never drink again, ever."

In Montgomery, Zelda spent time on the family porch where Scott had wooed her.

When a handsome couple strolled by the Sayre house, they smiled at her. She knew they were especially nice to her because, as everyone in Montgomery understood, she was a little touched.

"Good afternoon, Zelda."

She heard the word "sick" in the sky, in the trees, on the street. Then she heard the word "sick" spoken by the husband and wife, even though they were not speaking: "…sick… sick…."

Scott began a new novel with the same commitment he had given to *Gatsby*. He lay in bed and wrote in longhand on a pad. On the wall were the diagrams of plot and character movements.

Sheilah entered with soup and a sandwich.

"How's the novel?"

"This will be the best piece I've ever written."

"I'm glad."

"I'd love to see Hemingway's face when this comes out. It will kill him. Absolutely shatter him."

Sheilah smiled. "You'll show them."

"Thank you, Sheilo. Thank you for everything." Scott held Sheilah's hand. "Everything will change. I've changed. And if this is a success, I'd like to go to Europe and write about the war. Ernest won't have the field all to himself this time."

He rubbed his arms in discomfort before he rose and stepped out of the modest apartment bedroom.

Sheilah lounged on a sofa. She was reading a biography of Beethoven.

Scott sat in the corner recliner and picked up a Princeton alumni magazine. As he scanned it, he felt feverish and touched his warm forehead.

He bolted up like a shot, then braced himself against the

mantelpiece with his right hand and gripped his chest with his left. He fell spread-eagle to the floor.

"Scott. Scott!"

Choking, gasping sounds reverberated from Scott's throat. Sheilah frantically loosened his collar.

She rushed to the dinette and snatched a brandy bottle off it. She poured the liquid into Scott's clenched teeth, hoping it would revive him. The brandy rolled down his chin and neck.

It was too late. F. Scott Fitzgerald was dead of a heart attack.

He did not publish and receive rave reviews and show up Hemingway. *The Last Tycoon* was a brilliant novel, and it might have been a classic if he could have finished it. It's a tragedy he didn't live long enough to complete it. Orwell completed *Nineteen Eight-Four* on his deathbed, and though he didn't have the energy to finish editing it, he did live to see his greatest publishing success. Scott went out in similar fashion—having given his entire career to literature.

Zelda returned to the sanatorium, where a nurse escorted her to her quarters on the top floor.

"Good night."

Before leaving, the nurse locked Zelda in from the outside.

That evening a fire started in the kitchen and quickly spread by leaping up the dumbwaiter shafts to each room.

The stairways and corridors filled with smoke. The windows were shackled.

Was she asleep or did she pound on the walls? Her dark hair was cut in a stark fashion. She was small and frail. Bitterness distorted her beauty.

What did she say? "I'm locked in. Please, I can't get out. Help! Anyone!"

The fire overwhelmed the bed, curtains, carpet....

"Anyone."

Perhaps she began to pray. She certainly didn't deserve to die by fire. What had she done except marry an alcoholic, but brilliant writer? She was multi-talented and had turned religious in her last years. Did she travel too close to the sun? What was her sin, or are human beings so fragile that once broken, they remain that way? Or perhaps her death was a random accident, just bad luck that she was there.

In my imagination, Zelda's ending went something like this:

The fire engulfs her room. Zelda calmly rises and pushes open the door and walks out of the room.

When Zelda exits the hospital, she is the same age as she was when she first met Scott. Waiting for her is young Scott.

They hold hands and walk away from the burning hospital towards infinity.

Kristin B.

And thus, without a wing,
Or service of a keel,
Our Summer made her light escape
Into the beautiful.

Emily Dickinson

Part I: Kristin

I

IT WAS LIKE A SAW sliding inside, over and over.

The producer groaned and pumped. His heaviness punished her as if he were made of steel or a tense, obdurate negativity he'd absorbed over a lifetime. She suffocated beneath his groans, sweaty cologne, and prickly hairs.

All she could hear and feel was a roar, a thunder all around her. It appeared to be a part of her now as if she were wearing a helmet and a stone mask that circulated shock throughout her.

He gripped her arm and forced her into a small closet.

She sat in there, naked. Her hair bristled with static electricity against some clothes. She could hear him cleaning up in the front room. She covered her eyes when the door opened, and he intruded.

"Come on out."

"I want to go home."

His expression was pensive, tight, and guilty. He didn't have shoes on and his pale feet stunk out of his dress slacks. "Well, come on out."

She didn't move.

"Get up."

She forced herself to stand.

The lights were on now. The home/office was huge, with a bar, movie posters of the films he had produced, and several adjoining rooms.

A laptop, paper, and other items lay in a pile on the desk.

Kristin's warm hands covered her chest and groin area. She examined the hardwood floor. She took her shirt, skirt, and panties from him.

"Go into the bathroom and get cleaned up."

Kristin hurried in and pulled her clothes on, then splashed water on her lips and brushed back her hair.

In the mirror, her eyes were shiny and bloodshot, her cheekbones extremely pronounced.

She came out carrying one shoe.

He sat on the leather couch next to the other shoe. He examined her. "I'll give you a lift home."

She shook her head no. "I followed you here."

He appeared stoic for a beat, then, "If you call the police, I'll destroy you."

Kristin had lost all her energy. She shrank, unresponsive, in front of him.

The producer picked up her manuscript and leafed through it.

"*Young Scott and Zelda.* This is a great story and fine writing. I'll see what I can do."

"No."

The producer appeared hurt or angry as he shot her an intimidating glare, but he handed her the manuscript.

She took it from him and started to walk to the door. He picked up her shoe and gave it to her.

"I can't admit it," he said, burying his hand in his hair. "If you call the police, the best you could do is get me to settle out of court."

She didn't try to put on her shoes.

"I really don't want my lawyer to humiliate you."

"I just want to go home."

He flicked his wrist toward the door as if to dismiss her.

Outside, under the hot Los Angeles moon, she considered jumping on the 405 and driving out of town.

She crisscrossed the still-busy late-night LA traffic, from the Marina through Venice, up Olympic to her apartment on the Westside.

There were no parking places in the street, so she slammed on the brakes and pulled into the full tenants' lot, leaving her car in the middle, blocking everyone.

She stepped out and limped as fast as she could; sharp pain rotated through her restricted movement.

Inside, a hot shower beat down on her. The chaotic and steady roar continued and raced through her mind, focusing on the new sensibility that had kidnapped her spirit. She slept for a couple of hours on the edge of scattered dreams that later, before sunrise, when she tried to understand their searching quality, seemed empty.

It was dark outside, but she felt the coolness of the night wearing down into the dryness of the day.

Her room was a mess with clothes, books, papers, shoes, and makeup strewn everywhere.

A large photo of Edie Sedgwick dominated the wall above her bed.

A siren wailed down Santa Monica Boulevard.

The pillow became hot and wet, so she flipped it around, twisting her neck from side to side to loosen her torpid face and cheekbones. Her shoulders were locked up on her neck.

The sight of her one-page screenplay outline and the interested note on her desk from the producer made her convulse in hacking coughs. She wiped away the tears and read the outline that had drawn the producer's interest.

Twenty-one-year-old F. Scott Fitzgerald was a pretty boy, a drinker, remarkably outgoing for one so sensitive and, of course, gifted. It was during this period in his life that he fell madly in love with the beautiful, eccentric, and talented eighteen-year-old Southern belle, Zelda Sayre.

I have an intelligent, marketable, feature-length script that captures the complexity, beauty, and excitement of these two American legends.

The story line (quickly) is about Scott's last days at Princeton, where he is jilted by a wealthy debutante and told, "Poor boys shouldn't think of marrying rich girls." From Princeton, he enlists in the army during World War I and is stationed in Montgomery, Alabama. He meets Zelda and is immediately obsessed with her. She is equally attracted to him, and with some difficulty, he becomes her top beau.

When the war ends, they are secretly engaged, but before they can marry, Scott must prove that he will be able to support her. He moves to New York to make his fortune. He struggles, unable to sell his writing or find a well-paying job. After several months, the pressures of his lack of moneymaking possibilities force Zelda, who loves only Scott, but has been going out with others, to sensibly end their relationship. Scott is devastated and goes on a three-week drunken binge.

When he sobers up, he quits his job and moves back to his parents' house in St. Paul, Minnesota. In his third-story, barren bedroom, he writes *This Side of Paradise*. After Maxwell Perkins of Scribner pens that the novel has been accepted, Scott is ecstatic and runs through the streets of St. Paul, telling strangers and friends alike.

Renewed by his success, Scott returns to Montgomery to win Zelda back. It is not easy or simple, but he does. *This Side of Paradise* is published and tops the bestseller list in the US. Scott and Zelda marry on April 3, 1920.

She craved glamour just like Scott and Zelda did when they were young. And what was wrong with some beauty and romance? She didn't want to write about Scott and Zelda's alcoholism, mental illness, estrangement, or epic failures.

She just wanted to be inside a world of style and beautiful hair and lovely views of the sea and dinner parties and fascinating friends. She craved security as well; she had always been so cautious that she had few friends, preferring to wait until she found that new magical life and freedom she believed in. What she discovered was that she was a bald woman, with nothing but the silent roar and a vulnerable emptiness inside her.

Her roommate, Taron, switched on the light, startling her. "Your car is in the middle of the parking lot. What the hell happened?"

Kristin realized someone was repeatedly honking a car horn. She pointed to her keys. "Could you move it for me?"

Taron snatched the keys and jogged out.

Gripping her eyes shut, Kristin remembered that she had always been half a person, but now she was no one, no one at all, no one she recognized; there was so much empty space.

When Taron returned, she perched on the edge of Kristin's single bed. "I think you need to call the police," Taron said.

"No—it's done."

Taron, a former college basketball star, sneered, standing with her hands on her hips as if she were in foul trouble. "You have to go to the hospital."

"Why?"

"You have to. Something might be broken, and I hate to say it, but you'll need to be checked for venereal disease, pregnancy, and AIDS periodically in the next year. And you might change your mind about going to the police. You won't have a chance if you don't go now."

"Can you turn off the light?"

Taron touched her wet hair. "Did you take a bath or shower?"

"Yes."

"You destroyed all the evidence, Kristin!" Taron snatched a sweatsuit off a hangar out of the closet. "Come on, you have to do it. I'll take you."

At four or five in the morning, Kristin thought she would see the doctor right away, but the emergency room was a popular place for drama.

A thin, wiry-muscled black man flailed his long arms, whacking a nurse in the face, before a doctor and the nurse somehow managed to sedate him. A wide-eyed white woman just kept staring at Kristin.

"I can't believe how callous they are. You could be bleeding all over the place and they wouldn't notice," Taron said. "Some hospitals have rape units."

A nurse approached Kristin. "I need you to fill this out. Do you have insurance?"

When Kristin entered the room for treatment, she saw the nurse mouth "rape" to a doctor with black curly hair. The doctor didn't acknowledge the nurse.

"She took a shower," the nurse said.

"Kristin, if this was a rape, we have to call the police. If you want to say it was rough sex, we can treat you without calling the police," the doctor said.

"Can we talk about this later?" Taron asked.

"I'm sorry, you're going to have to wait outside," the doctor said.

Taron didn't leave.

"If it occurred, we need to report it. It's the law." He waited for an answer.

Taron looked like she wanted to say something, but held her tongue.

"It was rough sex," Kristin whispered.

"Jesus." Taron walked out.

The doctor and nurse glanced at each other and placed Kristin's legs in stirrups.

"Kristin, I'm going to have to check the vaginal area for blood or semen," the doctor said. Then, to the nurse, "Cut some hair for fibers and anything else."

The doctor swabbed her vagina. "Did he penetrate your rectum?"

Kristin wiped away her slow, burning tears. "No."

"Are you on birth control?"

"Yeah."

"Is your menstrual cycle regular?"

"Yeah."

"Were you a virgin?"

"Yeah, sure. I was a virgin."

He appeared confused by her sarcasm. The doctor looked at the nurse, who shook her head. "Check for fingernail scrapings. And test for acid phosphate to identify the blood type. Any external injuries to mention?"

"Minor bruises. A cut lip," the nurse said.

He ignored her lip.

"You'll need to be tested for HIV and other sexually transmitted diseases."

Kristin covered her face with one hand.

The next morning, Kristin called work and told them she had a family emergency. She had $3,600 in her savings account.

She finally left her apartment after three weeks, driving with Taron to Abbot Kinney Boulevard, an eclectic mix of style, art, and bohemia.

They sat in the bar near a window. She wore ripped jeans, a black T-shirt, and big dark glasses to hide the dark circles around her eyes.

Kristin crossed her legs and fell into her stringy hair and pale profile. She could barely hold herself up as she ventured down and in; the roar felt like a black hole pulling her into the darkness before she would be distracted and aggravated by any inconvenience. Even someone glancing at her or coming near caused a sharp hate to rise in her chest and harden her jaw.

She hated the young people that strolled by, carefree.

"I want you to buy something for yourself. It'll make you feel better. Or better yet, I'll buy you something," Taron said, "Something young and fun."

"Can I buy my stupid and innocent youth back? That's all I want."

"Youth is not for pleasure. It's for heroism."

"Who said that?"

"Paul Claudel."

"Camille's brother?"

"Yeah, the French poet."

She thought about French writers—Camus and Gide and Robbe-Grillet—and their books of random or confusing murders or alienation and the timeless strangeness of their imaginary worlds. This led to the South Americans and their reviews of books that have never been written, or life's labyrinths. "I don't think Paul was ever raped," she said. She wished she hadn't. She didn't even know what she meant. The sun flooded in behind her, burning the nape of her neck.

"What if he does it to someone else?" Taron asked, bordering on self-righteousness, before waving herself off with her left hand, perhaps not wanting to sound too critical.

"You heard the doctor. I need to take care of myself."

Kristin had lived in LA since she was eighteen. She had been isolated for long periods of time. With yoga, the beach, her writing, a nice roommate, a long trail of short-term boyfriends, and a job as an editor at an independent paper, she recently had been reasonably content, even if each day was like any other day. Now she had nowhere to go, but she needed to go somewhere. She felt pulled toward the simplicity of her sleepy, windy barbecue hometown thirty minutes north of Santa Barbara.

A young man in tight jeans and black boots, with long blonde hair, strutted past them as if he were God's gift to women.

They moved to a new spot where they were seated in a circular room filled with soft, exotic pillows. She drank several glasses of cold water. Taron sipped white wine. The room stank of incense and sandalwood.

"*The Last Tycoon* is the saddest book I've ever read."

Taron looked at her as if she had lost her mind. "Why do you say that?"

"It echoes the loss of Zelda in a great unfinished book by a great dying artist about a great dying artist."

"I saw the movie," Taron said.

"It would have been sweeter than *This Side of Paradise*."

A belly dancer appeared, gyrating her cotton candy-colored stomach.

"Did I tell you—I got my tape deck ripped out again?" Taron said. "This time they pried the trunk open with a crowbar."

Kristin's dash had been torn apart twice, so the casing where her tape deck slipped in could be stolen; the thieves needed it for their stolen tape decks.

The belly dancer rattled her charms above her head, swaying her hips out of the room.

Kristin avoided the constant gaze of a guy wearing too much makeup and pointed, silver-buckled shoes. He kept lifting his fedora, so his long, black curls fell into his eyes, before he tossed them back with a jerk of his head.

"I can't stay here."

Taron seemed to stare at nothing, as if she were lost.

II

A GAUNT KRISTIN sat in the middle of her Melrose wardrobe: leather jackets, miniskirts, bright or paisley vintage shirts, velvet pants, piles of black clothes from her teen years when she wore mainly black. More than forty-five pairs of shoes lay jumbled around the shoe cubbyholes. The only non-clothing items were her mother's jewelry, several boxes of disheveled literature (Oates, Spark, Le Guin) she had not touched since college, her yearbooks from three different high schools, and a newspaper clipping of her receiving a scholarship from the Lions Club.

Nineteen-eighties fashion was out of style all of a sudden. The imprisonment of her mind seemed to have oddly freed her from the past. The present was a swirling roar, but her years in Los Angeles were a thin line that connected her childhood to college to the present. Other than her fickle sense of fashion, the last ten years were just isolated afternoons.

She wasn't about to tow her past wardrobe back home, so she drove several carloads to Catholic Charities to donate.

At the relief center, a wrinkled woman with a happy smile

and boyish haircut examined her Doc Martens, silky dresses, paisley shirts, and pendants.

"These were expensive?" The lady smiled, holding up a pair of black boots.

"A couple hundred dollars."

The woman's smile never left her face, as if it were permanent. "We'll be able to sell these in a couple days to the kids that come in here."

On the morning Kristin packed up to return to her father's house, she almost felt lonely for the familiar desperation LA harbored.

"I didn't realize how desolate I'd feel when you were gone," Taron said, putting her arm through Kristin's.

"You have a lot of friends."

In contrast, she had only received two calls in the past two months—one from the clinic to tell her she had a clean bill of health, the other from an Edie Sedgwick-obsessed former roommate who had moved to New York to try to make it as a model. She wanted Kristin to loan her money.

"I'll have a room waiting for you if you change your mind," Taron said.

"It's going to be a while."

The lonely Westside blue skies reflected off cars and buildings as she picked up speed and curved along the 405 past Sunset. She turned up the Smiths on KROQ.

After bumper-to-bumper traffic in the Valley, she sped through Lost Hills and Thousand Oaks. Finally, near Camarillo, the undeveloped land, wide-open blue sky, and ocean breeze washed away her LA dehydration. A tremor of freedom sank into her soul.

Outside Santa Barbara, a man-made gilded island at the end of a short pier reminded her that her father had told her when she was ten years old that it was Gilligan's Island. She and her father used to listen to the radio; they didn't talk much. This flight of fancy by him was unusual, which is probably why she remembered it so clearly.

The island hadn't changed. It stretched out to the bending of the light. It was then that she inhaled the ocean air. And perhaps it was the sea scent that triggered the vivid memories.

The breeze chilled her shoulders, but she refused to stop to pull a sweater out and put it on. The freeway eventually curved inland, but the salty air sutured her swirling confusion.

She knew she was close to home—*Oh God, home.* She felt like she had accomplished something just by being able to drive back.

She turned left at the Kentucky Fried Chicken, then right down her sun-dappled street, lined with spacious, well-manicured homes inhabited mainly by families who had lived in Rio Madre their entire lives. All the houses seemed somewhat similar, but with enough individuality to make them unique. The common denominators: wide porches, white trim, bright gardens, and fragrant deciduous trees.

Passing the house, she made a U-turn to park in front, alongside the high curb. She could see her father's original 1965 aqua-blue Chevy Malibu shining in the long driveway.

Unlocking the door, she expected him to greet her in his helpful way, but he lay sprawled asleep on the recliner, a half-finished drink his companion.

She took the glass and buried her nose in the whiskey as if it were a fine wine. She downed it and savored the burning sensation circulating through her sunken lungs.

The TV was on—some game show. Kristin turned it off.

That evening, her father wore a brown sports coat and a white shirt. Along with his tentative manners, the coat made her imagine he was a wise gentleman scholar. He actually worked at the Vandenberg Air Force base, and she didn't really know what he did. His title was Engineer, but he never went to school for engineering. "I've cleaned your room," he said. "I didn't touch anything."

His movements had grown slower and his hearing had deteriorated since she last saw him, about a year earlier in Santa Barbara. His handsome face remained well preserved. Tears dripped down her cheek.

"Honey, what's the matter?"

"Nothing. Nothing's the matter."

"Is it boy trouble?"

His ignorance made her laugh and cough a little at the same time.

"No. LA didn't work out."

They sat in awkward silence, having run out of small talk.

"Are you planning to stay?"

"I don't know."

He hesitated, perhaps unsure whether his ideas were welcome, until she offered an opening.

"What could I do here?"

"You don't need a teaching credential to substitute. It's seventy-five dollars a day, I'm told, and you can choose your own days. I've always believed you'd make a wonderful teacher."

"Maybe," she whispered.

She considered this for a while, and the more she did, the more interested she became in being around kids. She wasn't sure how long it would take to feel up to doing this, but she might try it when she felt stronger—in a week or two or three. She didn't want to live off her father.

Her old bedroom was still full of posters of her high school faves—Joy Division, David Bowie, Blondie. The room seemed much smaller than it used to. She did not sleep well. She did not dream.

III

SHE READ IN BED until three or four in the morning; she rarely got up until after noon. In the early evening, she ventured to the video store, the grocery store, and the mall, for no particular reason except to be out of the house and to kill time.

She spent hours each day sifting through magazines, videos, and books at the library or in her room. On Saturdays, she went to evening mass with her father for Communion and for something to do. Her father beamed with pride when he introduced her to his fellow ushers, who greeted her from then on with esoteric smiles. She searched the pews for someone—anyone—she could make a connection with.

She didn't completely rebel against the Catholic Church. She particularly disliked most priests, who rarely inspired her and sometimes gave her the creeps. She hated the bishops, the fat-assed pharisees. She loved Christ, parts of the Mass, the architecture, the Virgin Mary, the Holy Spirit, and the sacrament of Communion. Communion felt pure to her the first time she took it, in second grade. Visiting the church when no one was in it soothed her spirit. It was within walking distance of her father's house, and she went in often. She sat in front of the Mona Lisa smile and satin purity of the Virgin Mary and the Cross. This was the highlight of her day—soaking in the forgiveness, redemption, and love of Christ's mother. She offered her sins and hatred to Christ and prayed to recover what she had lost.

From organized religion and the church, she received no laughter or joy, and often wanted to run from them as far as possible. She felt guilty, of course, as if it were her fault. She had tried Protestant churches in the past, but they were more singular and alienating. Some felt like high school pep rallies or political.

She soon learned what the unemployable, homeless, and raped do with their time. They hung out in the library, church, mall, and parks, just observing life go by while they thought about themselves, trying to blend in, afraid to trust anyone.

She saw them daily. Several of them scared her, especially two library dwellers—a crazy man with greasy hair and pants that hung low, and a large man with kinky, eraser-shaped hair and possessive eyes. "He's harmless," a librarian told her.

Not to me, she thought.

Her sole friends were books she had previously known only by reputation: *The Bell Jar, The Man Who Fell to Earth, Christiane F., De Profundis, Living Well is the Best Revenge*. The powerful conflicts, poverty, loss, and journeys in these works were her social life.

She loved her imaginary world where she spent her time alone and only one thing existed—happiness.

The holidays rolled by slowly. She and her father dined out on Thanksgiving (she still didn't eat much despite having shed twenty-five pounds off her slender frame). After opening their presents on Christmas Eve (she bought him a sweater; he got her gift certificates, perfume, and an electronic chess set she once mentioned), they watched a Swedish film she had rented.

By the middle of January, an anxiousness to be involved with someone, something, anything, dominated her depression. Early in February, she bumped into an acquaintance, Janet, from high school. Janet was a year older than she; they played together on the tennis team one year.

Browsing magazines in the mall bookstore, she was grateful when Janet treated her as if they were long-lost doubles partners.

"You know Kevin Helms of Helms Farms?"

She had never heard of either.

"It's taken a while, but we're going to tie the knot in three weeks in Santa Barbara," Janet said.

Kristin imagined that Janet's trusting and open personality came from living in a safe, small town all of her life and going out with the same guy since her sophomore year in high school.

"What are you doing now?"

"Waiting for my transcripts, so I can substitute teach."

"Where did you graduate?"

"UCLA."

"I didn't know that," Janet said. "In teaching?"

"Comparative Literature."

Janet made Kristin feel special. She had always felt as if it were her destiny to do something unique in her life. Even being so thoroughly humiliated confirmed her separateness.

Walking outside, Janet asked if she was married. "Everyone I know is married. There's Kevin's brother." Janet shook her bobbed hair as if she were shaking out the gall. "Of course, he was an addict and still seems strung out." She shrugged. "He's back at his mother's, sleeping till noon, surfing, doing nothing." She stepped back and looked Kristin up and down. "You've lost weight."

That night Kristin broke a sweat dancing in her room by herself, playing one of her favorite New Order songs over and over.

Afterward, breathless, she lay down with only enough energy to listen to music. She was going to be twenty-nine, and she still danced alone in her room as if she were fifteen. She had wasted too much time going to clubs and fucking lousy actors or no-bodies who thought they were James Dean, even when they rarely knew who Dean even was.

The following week she received an invitation to Janet Middleton's wedding.

When the wedding day arrived, Kristin decided to skip the ceremony and go to the reception late.

She arrived in time to get in line to greet the wedding party. As she waited, a short, stocky man decked out in cowboy boots, a yellow western-style shirt, and a horseshoe bolo sidled up behind her and smiled.

"Damn, this buck-ninety-nine champagne is classy stuff," he said. "Do you want me to get you a glass?"

"I'm not thirsty."

"I'm Milo."

Milo said he worked for Helms Farms as the sales manager. He had lived in Rio Madre his entire life, and when he discovered he didn't know her father, it seemed to disturb him.

"The town is getting too big now. Over fifty thousand," he said.

She hadn't noticed. She had been gone so long that it now reminded her of the two slightly larger Central Coast cities she grew up in. The towns ran together somewhat in her mind, as if they could all be the same place.

Across the hall, she observed the smiling bride and groom. A teenaged boy teased the groom for being shorter than he was. Kevin reacted by giving the boy a fake punch to the ribs.

Milo finished his champagne with one quick gulp. "You can tell Ms. Helms had a hand in this, can't you?" he asked, sweeping his arm out at the handsome hall, busy waiters, open bar, and elaborate stage. "She has money."

Leaving her books and bedroom seemed like a bad idea when she considered this character playing pocket pool beside her.

"It's her dough. The Middleton's don't have it, and it doesn't mean anything to her. At the rate she's going, Kevin's going to inherit this whole damn valley pretty soon."

Milo never took his eyes off Kristin, never took his left hand out of his pocket.

Almost everyone there seemed nice—nice families, nice young people—and she got stuck with this guy. It was just part of being a single woman, she knew, but she hated him, *really* hated him, and felt the nasty desire to see him dead. She smiled to herself at the thought.

She considered spinning around and marching out, but instead she focused on a couple with dark hair in the shadows to the left of the wedding party. They seemed peculiar and attractive sitting there, away from the light. As she edged closer in the slowly moving line to this quiet, alert couple, she gathered they were important, because those who spotted them turned back to greet them with eager bows, pleasant gestures, and respectful handshakes.

When she was close enough to get a decent look at them, a wreath of baby's-breath and white flowers blocked her view.

She forgot about the couple as she smiled into Janet's starry-eyed joy. "You look beautiful," she said.

"Honey, this is the friend I was telling you about." Janet tugged at her husband's tux sleeve. A much bigger man than Kristin had gauged from a distance, he was around six feet, with stiff hair and the ruddy coloring of a man who drove or walked through dusty fields and worked out in the sun.

He raised his eyebrows, and glanced down to his five ushers, making her feel uncomfortable. "Thank you for coming," he said.

"I'll call you when we get back from Hawaii," Janet said.

"I'm really happy for you."

After she shook hands with and quickly moved past the ushers, she had a clear view of the male half of the couple. His Milky Way complexion accentuated the eager angle of his face.

He seemed to smile, but it wasn't a real smile; it was as if he'd forgotten how to smile and was practicing the real thing. As she stumbled on, she caught the smoldering intensity of the not-so-young, but attractive, black-haired woman sitting next to him. She would have avoided looking her way, but the woman radiated something cold yet compassionate. Her mouth twisted downward as she stared at Kristin and didn't glance away.

Kristin sat with a very nice family and made polite small talk during the sirloin, salad, and beans dinner. After the toasts, she sauntered outside to the edge of the redwood deck. The pitch-blackness of the canyon in the starless, moonless night made her feel like she was somewhere in the middle of the sky, unable to distinguish which way was up.

She spotted him sitting alone, staring into the same confusing sky, as if he were unaware that a party beat on behind them.

He stood, making several uncomfortable gestures with his hands and feet before stepping around the table toward her.

He moved with athletic grace in his slender suit. He was only as tall as she was.

"I've been wanting to meet you. I'm Kevin's brother, Holden," he said.

He held her hand for a beat.

"You were a baseball player?"

"It's been a while. You're a tennis player?"

Janet must have told him. "I haven't played tennis since high school."

He surveyed the ground, then gazed through the sliding glass doors that distorted the figures inside.

She glanced in at the dancers and imagined her cheek brushing his and his clean, soft fragrance enveloping her. His shoulders and waist would be hard where she placed her hands.

"You don't seem like a baseball player."

"I never did."

She worried that she had said the wrong thing. "I'm sorry, I have to get off that subject."

"It doesn't matter."

She wondered if it did matter until she saw Milo barreling across the dance floor toward them.

"Who is that man?" She leaned toward Holden, but Milo was there before he could answer.

Milo appeared grim. "Holden, you're wanted up front for some photos." Milo did not look at him. Holden pressed his lips together, perhaps in dissatisfaction.

"Tell them I'll be there in a few minutes."

"They want you there now."

Holden turned his back to Milo. Milo glared at Holden from behind him for a moment, then marched away.

"I think I'm going to leave," she said.

"Now?"

"I'm really exhausted."

Her sudden departure seemed to deflate them both. They began to walk together in silence.

She and Holden said goodbye, but before they did, they just stared at each other for a few seconds. His hazel eyes searched right through her light and her emptiness.

IV

THE PLEASANT WOMAN who organized the school district's substitute teachers' phone calls woke Kristin each morning for two weeks to request her to substitute.

Her first day began with a wonderfully sweet second-grade class. Her biggest problem was botching the morning routine. "Ms. Boyd, we have to put up what day it is." By three o'clock, she had made thirty little friends.

After school, the wind surprised her with its force, blowing through the broccoli and lettuce fields. Kids were everywhere—on bikes, in groups, being picked up by their parents.

She kept her head angled down against the invisible pressure.

"If there was one thing I would change about this area, it would be the wind. It drives people crazy." Holden Helms glided up the slight slope from the curb to the school. The blue pickup truck haphazardly parked across the street must be his, she guessed. A surfboard jutted out of the pickup bed. "How was school? I bet the kids love you."

She frowned into the wind. "They're sweet."

He examined the ground as if he were no longer sure of himself now that he was so close to her. It was an odd, shy gesture that she assumed was a habit. She believed he acted a certain way because he understood its charming effect on others.

"How did you know I was here?"

"I called your house. Your father told me you were subbing," he said. Shuffling his feet, he pivoted toward the wind and mumbled, asking if she was seeing anyone. "What I'm trying to say is that I'd like to take you out."

Sometimes he seemed as if he had no self-confidence, as if he were uncertain of everything he did.

At home, her father sat up and set his paper down when she told him she was going out with someone. "I'm glad, honey."

She wondered if he had heard of Holden since he devoured the sports page daily. "His name is Holden Helms! He used to be a professional baseball player!" she shouted from her bedroom, before shuffling out in her stocking feet, so he would not have to shout back.

"Yes, I know who he is."

"Tell me what you've heard. Tell me what you know." She didn't recognize herself being so carefree.

Her father crooked his head, as if weighing his words. "He was a talented athlete but had personal problems. He's still very young. He might be younger than you." He slouched down to focus on his magazine.

She went to her room when he didn't elaborate, disappointed

that her father knew about Holden's troubled past. She lay on her stomach and stared through the slits in the venetian blinds at the sunlight darting across the lawn. The wind brushed the grass and swirled the leaves.

On Saturday night, when the doorbell rang, she listened to her father invite Holden in.

Taking one last glimpse in the mirror, she liked what she saw—a college graduate, a substitute teacher, and a fair-haired girl with a mysterious date. She was like anyone going out on Saturday night—except for having to fight the desire to remain in and read.

Hearing their voices, she couldn't help but listen.

"I read several American League teams were interested in signing you," her father said.

She imagined Holden looking down.

"A couple teams called, but I'm not really that interested."

After saying good-bye to her father, she climbed into Holden's pickup. Inside, the seats and dash were polished and slick. It smelled of mint. Holden closed the door behind her.

In the sunken Wine Cellar, soft lights, shadows, and aging bottles of wine surrounded them.

After a peppery glass of Santa Barbara Pinot, she had divulged little. He didn't seem to mind and leaned close to her over the corner edge of the table.

"You know, I have this thing about people," he said. "If I

touch them, it's as if I can tell right away if a person is going to be someone special in my life." He leaned back and pressed two fingers against his sanguine lips. "I thought there was something between us when we shook hands on the terrace."

She examined his scarred, sharp knuckles. "Well, go on and fill me in on this magic of yours. I'm intrigued to hear how it works."

His eyes reflected the gold Spanish tiles. "For example, this black guy, a little older than me, comes in late and sits in the empty chair next to mine in my first week in the majors. For some reason I slapped him on the back, and from that moment on, I knew we would be close friends."

Kristin thought his smile was intoxicating, particularly because he didn't smile much.

"Does any of this make sense? I've never told anyone that before." His cheeks flushed red, perhaps embarrassed.

It made sense, she thought, watching him sip his wine. They were at a place where small events or gestures were important. "I understand what you're saying. I believe people come into your life for a definite reason."

Before she could finish her thought, a large man invaded their intimacy.

"Holden Helms?"

She had seen him when they walked in. He had been talking with a group, and they became quiet when Kristin and Holden entered. This man's deep voice contained a threat of concealed belligerence. His oppressiveness overwhelmed her.

"Mr. Helms, me and my nephew went to see you play when

you were in LA. He worshipped you, man." He set his thick hands down on the table. His nasal voice echoed in the cellar.

"I appreciate that." Holden sat motionless, while the man seemed to puff up, hotter and hotter.

"You appreciate nothing, you overpaid, spoiled prima donna."

Holden's eyes grew piercing and light green. "Look, that's ancient history. I'm just having a private drink."

From behind the bar, the bartender appeared, drying a glass. "Frank, knock it off," she said, in a scratchy voice.

Frank focused on Kristin. "What are you doing with this loser?"

She didn't respond except to get up and hurry past the bartender, who moved out of her way.

"Leave her out of this," Holden said.

She pushed open the lobby's heavy brass door, swinging into the noisy coolness of the night. She took several abortive steps, trying to remember where he had parked.

Out of breath and a little confused, she was standing in the middle of the parking lot when she spotted Holden's truck. The lights from the hotel tracked down on her as she fell against it and waited, feeling too small to walk home.

Holden appeared at her side. "Are you all right?"

"No."

"He's just a drunk."

Shouts coming from the hotel broke the silence. She heard the man bellow, "Fuck you!" to the lobby. The same phrase was returned to him.

Holden exited through the lot entrance, perhaps to avoid the man wandering in their direction.

Holden turned on to the freeway toward Santa Barbara. They hadn't spoken and the silence became uncomfortable. She wasn't going to say anything, and she appreciated it when Holden began speaking about himself.

"We own land right past those orange groves," he said, pointing to several lights that, if they were closer, would have been bright.

"That's your family's property?"

"As far as you can see."

She wished she could say something cheerful or witty, but her mind seemed to be in a deep freeze. She felt the constant tug to remain in her room and avoid people. She was no Zelda. She would never be the life of the party, a carefree belle or a flapper.

She focused on the music coming from Holden's stereo.

"Did you mix this?" she asked, when a David Bowie song began.

"Yes. Do you like it?"

"Yes."

"Are you upset about what happened back there?"

"Yes."

"I'm sorry. I can't believe that happened. It's never happened before."

"He reminded me of the man who raped me seven months ago."

"Oh, Jesus." Holden pulled the truck over. "Is he in jail?"

"I don't want to talk about that."

Driving on State Street by the fine houses and condos sheltered by shady trees, Holden turned through a residential area before hitting the clearing and the grounds of the lovely Santa Barbara Mission.

Lights above the tiled rooftops reflected off the shimmering goldfish in the fountain. He gave her a quarter, and they made wishes and flipped the coins over their left shoulders. Hearing the "kerplunk," she twisted back to watch her coin's twinkling descent until it joined the mosaic of change that layered the bottom. Legend said that your wish would be granted on this sacred ground.

Holden pulled out a 35 mm camera. He snapped a few photos of the beautiful Mission and her.

That night, in the darkness of her room, she could hear the click of a glass and a bottle downstairs.

She could not sleep, remembering Holden gazing up at the cross and the silver horizon below the topaz sky, leaning against the long canal where the monks, or perhaps it was the Indians, washed their clothes. The half-moon seemed as if she could touch it, and she asked Holden to tell her what he wished for, but he wouldn't say because then it might not come true.

She tossed and turned in bed, trying to think only of the romantic Mission, the boats blinking in the harbor. Still, nothing could help her escape the emptiness and the roar. Those moments of lightness made her realize that her jaw felt locked up, and that she was still so shoved within herself, her soul so humiliated.

V

SHE SAT AT THE KITCHEN TABLE next to her father, who was
reading the *Rio Madre Times* sports page.

"How was your date?" He didn't glance up.

"He's a really nice guy."

He lifted his chin and turned a page. "Just be careful. I don't
know how kids can get hooked on drugs with all the informa-
tion available to them."

She stared across the table, wanting to ridicule him for what
he did not know, but she felt too guilt-ridden to speak.

The Sunday morning sky was enormous, aqua blue, and free of
clouds and wind. She had to get out of the house, so she called
Holden, who suggested they go to the shooting range. It was an
out-of-the-blue suggestion, but it struck her that he was trying
to help her escape her fears, so she agreed.

He sauntered up the narrow cement walkway, carrying a soft,
small leather pouch.

Pushing off her bed, where she had been waiting and watching, she went to the door.

"Hi."

She invited him in, and they sat on the couch, listening to her father raking leaves in the backyard.

"Is everything all right?" Holden asked.

"Yes," she said, as if she didn't know why he asked.

Her eyes shifted from his leather pouch to the yellow wallpaper and the piano in the corner, which neither she nor her father knew how to play.

"It's not windy today," Holden said.

"It will probably come up later."

He nodded as if that were all right with him.

"Did you bring it?"

He patted the leather pouch. "You ready to do this?"

She didn't answer.

"You don't have to."

"I'm ready."

She didn't say another word in the car. She wondered if he thought she was crazy, as she frequently checked the rearview mirror. He didn't turn around until she did it again when they reached the shooting range—nothing there but empty road.

She could hear the shots before they reached the entrance. She was wearing baggy cargo pants, a sweatshirt, and a baseball cap to appear as unfeminine as possible.

It was almost all men and boys. Lots of Wranglers, Levi's, plaid shirts, and trucker or cowboy hats. Not a lot of talking, but occasional male laughter broke through the gunshots. Not one person bothered her or ogled.

"I have two revolvers," Holden said. "This one shoots .38s and .357s, and this one 9 mm. A .38 or .357 is going to give you a kick—start with the 9 mm."

She nodded. "Have you been out here much?"

"It's been a long time."

"Your mother bring you out here?"

"No." His voice rose and his frown expressed disbelief. He caught himself and loaded the guns. "My father used to take us out here all the time. He liked guns."

"Do you?"

"No."

"I don't either."

She lined up, pressed both hands on the gun, and aimed with her eyes and feet in unison. Holden adjusted her.

BAM BAM BAM. They all appeared to hit the target.

"You didn't tell me you shot before."

"I've never shot a gun in my life." She smiled, pointing the gun toward the sky.

They went through several rounds. Her roar subsided. Her shoulders felt released from her neck.

On the way home, Holden stopped on a hilltop overlooking vineyards. The wind rustled, whipping across the outlining trees.

"It's nice to see you smile," he said.

She looked down at his shoes and kicked the dry dirt.

"Getting out of myself was a good idea."

"You're a totally different person from the one I picked up an hour ago."

She could still hear the gunshots. *BAM BAM BAM.*

She made a false motion with her lips, as if she wanted to say something else. She halted and turned toward the shooting range that blocked the wind. "You have to know something about me. I have nothing to give."

He stood straight and his eyes dilated. "You've given me a reason to get up in the morning. You've changed me. I'm ashamed of things I've done in the past."

"What kind of things?"

"Just being a stupid lustful teen."

"Did you rape anyone?"

"No, of course not."

She wasn't sure she wanted to know more; she couldn't deal with someone else's regrets or mistakes.

The scent of lime swept from the trees over them.

"This is a big thing for me to get out like this," she said.

On the way to a mall, she made him stop at the Catholic church.

Kaleidoscopic marble steps led from the street to the entrance of the complex, geometric, red brick building. The sunlight shone through the stained-glass stations of the cross on the right and the saints on the left.

Flowers and candles casting lovely shadows and light added to the artistic sense of spirituality, filling her void.

Holden sat in a pew as Kristin kneeled and prayed. Kristin crossed herself, then sat back and wiped away several tears. They didn't speak for a few minutes. When they did, it was in a whisper.

"It's funny that you don't have a father and I don't have a mother. I've always wondered what my life would have been like if I'd had one. If I would have been popular or the life of the party at baby or bridal showers. I don't quite understand what it is I don't know." She paused, wanting a comment from him. He said nothing. "I don't think about it too much," she continued. "It's just that intangible quality that most women have. Maybe it's confidence."

"Yeah," he said, as if he knew what she meant.

She wasn't sure if he agreed or understood or had had the same experience somehow. "What about you? When did your father pass away?"

"In 1979," he said. "Kevin looks just like him now. I never saw him again after I aimed one of his pistols at him. I really thought I was going to kill him. My mom had a nasty black eye. He was standing over her when I came in with the gun. If my mother hadn't stepped in front of him, he would have died that night instead of eight years later, choking on his own puke in a motel. He looked at me and he knew I was ready to pull the trigger. He stormed out the door, started up his pickup, and we never saw him again."

She was eleven when she discovered an old newspaper in her father's sweater drawer, she explained. It was opened to the second page and her eyes were drawn to the slender column on the left. She used to be able to recall it verbatim. "Cuesta Grade Victim Identified," it was titled. "Mrs. John Anthony Boyd apparently lost control on Cuesta Grade and slid across a center divider. Mrs. Boyd was driving home after working a late shift at Valley Hospital"…something like that.

Kristin would never have a complete childhood, and now was left with a blank canvas with no restrictions on her.

"His name was Harry. Harry Helms," Holden went on.

When they exited the church, a red sun hung over the ocean.

From the church they walked to the bustling mall.

In a fluorescent-lit store, she admired a silky white shirt she thought she might want to buy, when a female voice cheerfully called out "Holden!" It was his mother; her black hair was neatly combed high and back. Kristin hadn't seen her since the wedding. Holden resembled her up close.

Ms. Helms approached Holden with a clenched smile, kissing him on the cheek.

"I've been wondering where you've been spending all your time lately," Ms. Helms said, glancing at Kristin.

Holden shrugged with his hands.

"Aren't you going to introduce me to your friend?" Ms. Helms asked, after a moment of shifting silence.

"This is my friend, Kristin," he said.

"It's a pleasure to meet you," Ms. Helms said.

Kristin shook Ms. Helms's soft hand.

"I've seen you before, haven't I?" Ms. Helms asked, displaying a row of lovely white teeth.

"I was at Kevin's wedding. I went to high school with Janet."

"That's right," Ms. Helms said.

It struck her that Holden must have told his mother that she had been raped.

"It's so nice to meet you," Ms. Helms said, still smiling at her son.

Kristin stared at the white shirt.

"Why don't you come to dinner some time?"

"What about tonight, Mom?"

"I can't tonight," Kristin said.

Holden and his mother spoke for a few more minutes before Kristin watched his mother pivot and weave out to the aisle. She felt as if she were in some kind of walkabout as she stroked the silky white shirt.

"Did you set this up?"

"What do you mean?"

"Did you know she was going to be here?"

"No."

She circled the rack. "I know you told her."

He placed his hand on her shoulder, then removed it. "You can trust her."

"Don't ever do that again. She sees right through me and it's humiliating." A violent edge ached in her voice. "I need a little peace. That's why I came back to this little town...to see if I could recover myself." Her mind began to swirl.

"I want to help you do that," he said.

"I'm the only one who can help me."

At her father's house, moths flickered around the porch light as they reached the front door.

"I'll call you tomorrow," he said.

She looked down at his tennis shoes, then up at him, unsure she wanted him to call her. "I'm exhausted."

"Me too."

"I mean…it's hard for me to be around people."

"If anyone bothers you, I'll kill him."

The serious arcs of his cheekbones made her believe he meant it.

"I'm not sure we should see each other for a while."

VI

KRISTIN WOKE WITH A STARK SENSE of time running out, an impatience to be somewhere she belonged. She considered not substituting that day, but with nothing else to do, she worked an uneventful—bordering on maddening—day at a junior high. The absent teacher left the same lesson plan and test for the six rotating classes, prompting identical complaints.

"She always gives us open-book tests."

"Not this time."

"Oh, come on."

"Can I go out and get a drink of water? My throat is dry."

"Yeah, me too. It's hot outside."

"No."

"You're mean. I could have some kind of disease or be dying or something."

"As long as you survive to the end of the period."

"God, you're cold."

The day dragged on.

The next week she couldn't handle subbing and claimed to have the flu.

I can't do this isolation thing again, she begged herself, wondering where people garnered the strength to pull through the kind of malignant river of loss that seemed to always be flowing in her.

After Holden called three days in a row, she made her father tell him not to call again. Several times she saw him drive by her father's house.

It bothered her that he wanted to get inside her life, mind, and spirit. At other moments, she wished she were with him. One disturbing thought kept returning to her; she kept fantasizing Holden killing the producer. It gave her a sense of atonement. Sometimes she almost skipped around the house, believing he would do that.

It was similar to the freedom that she felt after she sent out the *Young Scott and Zelda* screenplay, when she believed every day an acceptance letter would be coming in the mail and her life would be changed forever. Deep down she wondered if she deserved it, or had the pull, talent, nerve, courage, and strength to get what she wanted.

She didn't know what she wanted now, but she decided to drive out to see Holden.

His dusty pickup was parked beneath a palm tree. A dirt

road led behind the white two-story house to a row of large red barns, sales offices, mechanical shops, coolers, packaging sheds, tractors, and water trucks. Farmers wearing blue-and-white Helms Farms hats came and went from the offices. The ocean wind slammed everything as it raged in the afternoon, pushing the scents of the sea and the miles of strawberry fields east.

She flipped around near his truck and came back to the blacktop. She parked in front, wondering what she would say.

The front door's thick, dark wood hurt her knuckles when she knocked. No answer. She rang the doorbell several times and listened to it echo.

A six-wheeled black truck stopped at the side of the house. She waited at the top of the stairs, shading her eyes from the sun. Dressed in Ropers and a plaid shirt, Milo jumped out.

"Hey."

She walked down the steps and around the rocks.

"It's you."

"I'm looking for Holden. Do you know where he is?"

"I'm not his keeper." He leered toward the distant mountains, then at her. "You look like you could use a drink."

"Do you know when he'll be back?"

"Nope."

Shifting from one leg to the other, she crossed her arms, afraid. "Could you tell him I came by if you see him?"

"He doesn't care about nobody."

He followed her to her car. "Come over to the office. It's got a great view of the valley and anyone coming or going. You can wait up there. Come on, we'll have a drink. It's dusty and windy out here."

"I gotta go," she said, jogging away.

"Some other time, beautiful."

She shifted into first gear and drove by him. He stood with his hands on his hips, his chin jutting out as if he were pleased with himself.

She made it home and called Holden. No answer. In her room, she picked up Fitzgerald's *Tender Is the Night* and plopped down on the bed. She attempted to read, but she didn't have enough concentration to get past the lovely first pages.

At dinner, she ate little of the aromatic seasoned corn on the cob her father had grilled. "I'm sorry, Dad. I'm not hungry," she said, excusing herself from the table.

"Are you feeling all right?"

"I'm fine." She could see how concerned and decent he was, but she couldn't tell him.

At ten-thirty, the phone rang. No one else called this house, let alone this late. She knew it had to be him.

"Kristin?"

"Taron," she said, hiding her disappointment.

"Did I wake you? You've really been on my mind tonight."

Taron gushed on with good news about her artwork. She

mixed and merged painting, sculpting, and photography. She had a large write-up in the *LA Weekly* that she was going to send to Kristin. "I see where I'm at in art history," she said.

Kristin never mentioned or hinted at Holden.

"Now I have some good news for you. Are you ready?"

"Why not?"

"I was introduced to this Australian film director who likes my work," Taron's voice rose from low to exuberant. "We've had dinner a couple times and have really hit it off. I showed her your script and gave you the big build-up, naturally. She read it and thinks it's wonderful. She said you have a lot of talent. I don't know what it means, but she's visiting in about a week. I'll see if she can recommend it to someone or how we can help you."

Kristin sounded excited for Taron's sake, but after she hung up the phone, she didn't believe anything would come of it. She could use the money. It would fund grad school and perhaps she would become a professor.

She remembered her deep love for *The Great Gatsby*, *The Last Tycoon*, and Fitzgerald's great gift for prose and romance. He wrote *Gatsby* when he was twenty-five or twenty-six, three or four years younger than she. That's why she had written the screenplay about Scott and Zelda.

Late the next morning, she marched obedient third graders to the cafeteria, where a barefoot instructor in a purple leotard gave them a modern dance lesson.

The children stretched and laughed as the teacher broke into a trot, shaking her short auburn hair.

Kristin waved good-bye and started walking back to the classroom when she saw Holden approaching.

His shoulders and face seemed thinner as if he hadn't been eating. He glanced at her, then looked at the ground; underneath his nervousness, she sensed his beating chest. He made a vague gesture to embrace her, but did not continue when she kept her arms crossed. Her hands opened and closed, and she pushed them deeper into her armpits.

He came near her, touching the nape of her neck beneath her hair. "Your footsteps are all over my heart," he said.

She kept her arms folded, fighting tears. "I know."

The next two weeks were the happiest she could remember. They spent every day together, going for walks, sending for food, and holding hands.

They walked on the beach several times and Holden even convinced her to let him try and teach her to surf.

She objected at first. "I don't swim. I'm terrified of my head going under the water."

She ventured out no deeper than her chest to ride the white water, close to the shore, which was sort of like boogie boarding. She kept trying to stand up, but she couldn't pop up fast enough and kept losing her balance and falling into the shallow water, which panicked her to keep her head above the water, but she still smiled each time she rose out of the water because she was trying get out of herself.

It was in this frame of mind that she received a call from Janet Helms. "I can't believe you're dating Holden," Janet said. "You both have to come over to the house this weekend for a little barbecue."

On the way to Janet and Kevin's ranch, Holden sped down an isolated road that led to Highway 1. They were surrounded by the gold coast of lettuce, strawberry, and cabbage fields that ran along like long, thin legs.

"Do you ever think that you can catch up with time?" Holden asked. "I mean…" He stared straight ahead as if he were on the verge of some discovery he was not sure how to describe. "You know, when the past ends and a new life begins? I keep seeing the number twelve on clocks all day long—2:12, 4:12, 7:12, 1:12, 11:12. I'll roll over in bed, and it'll be 12:12, like it's midnight in my life and a new day or time is beginning."

She was not sure what to say.

He raised his eyebrows as if waiting for her to comment. He smiled. She laughed and put her hand on his arm.

"I really do see twelve every time I look at my watch or clock."

A powder-blue Mercedes with the license plate JHELMS and a six-wheeled Chevrolet truck were parked in the Helmses' driveway.

At the door, Janet, wearing a white, full-length western-style dress, allowed her right hand to hang limply as she greeted them.

From the house, Kristin turned back to the Rio Madre valley, taking in the green and brown hues of the fields and the black snake of a road winding off into nothing.

"Well, you made it," Janet said.

Janet hugged her before giving them both a toothy grin.

Inside their home, a tasteful country twang ran through the oak vitrines, étagères, bookcases, and fireplace. A lovely photograph of a lonely trail leading up to a red-and-white farmhouse hung above the mantelpiece.

Janet's low heels tapped against the hardwood floor as she directed Kristin and Holden to the backyard.

"Just in time," Kevin said, pouring beer over two chunks of meat. Smoke and a hickory scent from the large pit rose up to the eucalyptus trees. Dressed in jeans and a plaid shirt, Kevin stood in front of Kristin. "How do you like your tri-tip? Well done? Medium?"

"I don't eat meat."

"Are you a vegetarian?" Janet wondered.

"Yes," she said.

Kevin frowned and picked up a long fork and examined the slab of meat. "Not too much longer." Setting the fork down, he gestured to Holden to go with him. "Let me show you what I'm doing back here, Holden."

Kristin began to follow, but Janet held her arm. "Let's go

inside. There's nothing out here. You don't want to see the cement he mixed."

Inside, Kristin sat on a soft sofa as Janet poured two full glasses of white wine.

"Well, tell me. How did it happen? How did you and Holden get together?"

Wine dripped outside Kristin's glass. "We met at the reception and became friends." She thought Janet would find a towel or napkin for her, but she ignored it.

"I could have been blown over by a feather, at first," Janet said, "but after I thought about it a little, you two are perfect for each other. You know, you're both so quiet." She turned her hand and wrist in unison. "Don't you think?"

Kristin hated when anyone said she was quiet. It made her feel like an oddball. "We're compatible."

"I'm so glad, and so is Kevin. You must know that you're the reason Kevin let me invite both of you here today." Janet drew near as if to tantalize her with the ambiguous compliment. "He thinks you're the best thing since sliced bread. I was a little jealous when I heard him tell his mother that on the phone the other day. I think it's wonderful, too. I mean, Holden's twenty-eight, and you're twenty-nine, right?"

"In August."

"You're a Leo and he's a moon child. That's special—the king and queen. Kevin thought you'd help Holden become a little more normal…or sociable, I think he meant. Don't you think?"

She listened to Janet's fluttery high voice, inflected to add emphasis. Kristin liked Janet and thought she was a genuinely nice person, but Kristin's face began to feel hard and withdrawn.

Kristin heard Holden and Kevin's footsteps before they appeared, clutching Budweiser longneck beers.

"Do you have everything ready in the kitchen?" Kevin seemed to eye his wife with distrust. "All I have left is the bread and that only takes a few minutes."

Janet stood, and she followed Kevin toward the kitchen. "I think we're ready," she said.

Kristin sank into the couch, happy to be alone with Holden, who leaned over the couch behind her. He gazed at her. He loved her, she knew. It made her shiver; she was so used to isolation. What was it like being exposed to someone day in and day out, she wondered?

"What did you two talk about?"

"Us."

He bent down in front of her. "We don't need other people."

"Are you two getting along all right?"

"Kevin's sauced. I guess they were expecting us a couple hours ago. They thought we weren't going to show up, for some reason."

"I'm sure she said five o'clock." Kristin tried to remember the conversation on the phone.

"Don't worry about it."

He smiled and put his hands, cold from the beer bottle, on hers.

She heard a faint sound of rustling or something grinding, maybe a dishwasher or blender, from the back of the house. "I love the colors and composition of that photograph."

His face twisted into a lopsided grin. "That's mine. My mother gave that to them."

"Hello," Ms. Helms said, smiling in the hallway entrance.

Holden stood up. "Hey, I didn't hear you come in."

"I only have time to say hello. Hi, Kristin."

Kristin admired Ms. Helm's strong presence.

"Are you staying for dinner?" Holden asked.

"I'm sorry. I just have time to drop some paychecks off to your brother. We'll get together soon, I hope." She offered a worried smile to Kristin before clicking away down the hall.

"She came by to spy on us," Holden said. "What can I say? You only have one mother."

Kristin stared at her interlocked fingers.

"I'm sorry. I completely forgot."

"I know you didn't mean anything." She stood up.

"Where're you going?"

"I'll be right back."

Walking down the hall, she found Janet standing against the wall, waiting. As she neared, she became aware of the voices outside.

"Don't let them see you," Janet said, pulling her back from the screen.

She caught a glimpse of Ms. Helms getting into a long, dark luxury car. Kevin held the door. She heard it slam.

"What's going on?" Kristin asked.

"That's what I want to find out," Janet whispered.

Kristin heard Kevin ask, "Why don't you stay? Why?" She couldn't hear Ms. Helms's response.

"Why wouldn't I be nice to her?" Kevin asked, throwing up his arms.

Kristin had heard enough and found the bathroom at the end of the hall.

When she returned, Ms. Helms had left. Janet stood behind Kevin with an empty plate in her hand. Holden waited off to the side. Two charred Portuguese sausages were pushed to the end of the grill. Kevin stabbed the links with the long fork, causing the fat to drip and sizzle into the white wood in the grill. Smoke rose up like a nuclear cloud before it dwindled into nothing.

"It's ready," Kevin said in a matter-of-fact tone, to no one.

The dinner table was crammed with steaming corn on the cob, aromatic pinto beans with strips of bacon, seasoned meats, and a salad bowl of lettuce, tomatoes, red cabbage, broccoli, and carrots.

Kevin smiled at Kristin, then took a long guzzle of beer.

Kevin held court, lecturing them on the politics of agriculture, several deceptive clean water propositions, and how the Helmses bought up bankrupt farms and turned them into profitable operations. "Hey, I'm not for subsidies. I've never taken a cent from the government."

Holden gave her a gaze of encouragement as Kevin continued to talk.

The phone rang.

"I'll get it," Janet said.

Standing as she spoke, Kevin threw his napkin on the table and picked up his beer. "I got it," he said, looking disturbed at this small intrusion.

"Is everything all right?" Janet asked, after Kevin left the room.

"Fine," she said.

She could hear the wind howling in from the ocean. Looking out the window, she realized she should probably socialize, but she just didn't want to small talk.

Janet began to ask her a question, but stopped when Kevin's conversation filtered in. "No, I don't understand," he said. Then, after a brief silence, "All right! All right! All right!"

"The table setting and food. It's all great," Holden offered.

Janet smiled, but Kristin could see her softly chewing, trying to listen to Kevin. Kristin believed she noticed Janet's dislike for Holden in her fake smiles and her quick thank-you.

"Whatever you say," Kevin said, just before he slammed down the phone. He didn't come directly back to the table, but soon reappeared, popping open a fresh beer.

"Who was that, honey?" Janet asked.

"Mom."

"What did she want?"

"She's worried about her little boy."

Kevin's receding, bristly hair stuck out as he kept pulling at it. His high forehead crested white where he normally wore a hat, the rest of his face reddened by the sun.

In front of Kevin, ugly brown spots trailed across the white tablecloth and all around the bean bowl. "I'll need to bleach this out," Janet said.

"Goddamn it, I forgot to call the cooler," Kevin groaned, twisting his mouth toward the window before he swigged his beer. "You wouldn't know anything about that or what Mom and me do out at the farm." He glared at Holden.

Holden leaned back as if to show he was not hiding anything. Holden could pass for a teenager, young and clean. Kevin was beat-up, his skin damaged, as if he never used sunblock. Holden was lithe. Kevin was pudgy. Kevin seemed to shrink from Holden.

"I think you could work in the cooler. You wouldn't have to be out in the sun and wind so it wouldn't hurt her prodigal son."

"K—Kevin?" Janet stammered.

"He lives rent free. He might as well earn it," Kevin said to his wife, as if daring her to prove him wrong. "He owns one-third."

"Kevin," Janet said again.

Holden gave Kristin a sidelong glance of embarrassment. She had the feeling he held back because she was present.

"I'm not a farmer," Holden said.

Janet announced she would clear the table, but first she rubbed the trail of bean spots for a moment with a napkin.

An incredulous Kevin gaped at his wife.

"You've never worked a goddamn day on the ranch in your life," Kevin said, hunching further sideways as if it protected him.

A fork slipped off the plate Janet held and clanked against a glass. She set the dishes down. "Can I talk to you in the kitchen?" she asked.

"Not one day," Kevin prodded, as if his wife had set him off again. "Never had to try and get people to care about him. Never went to school. Never did shit, except fuck himself up so bad he has to live at home at twenty-eight."

Kevin stopped because Holden stood and pushed his chair down. Holden tried to raise his voice, but it quivered, stunted by anger. He did not seem to be practiced in the art of verbal argument. "What more do you want, Kevin? I have all my money. I take care of myself."

"In a fucking savings account."

"It's all there."

"Why don't you tell me why Mom's acting so strange about you two? Why don't you tell me what the secret is you're hiding now? You and Mom are always hiding things from me."

"It was his fault, Kevin. It was his fault," Holden said.

She thought for a moment that Kevin would hurl himself across the table at his brother. Instead, he dropped his napkin and marched out. "I'm not talking about him."

Outside, Holden refused to speak. In the car, he shifted gears with authority, zipping and weaving through the back roads, driving too fast, and swerving around corners, ditches, and banks of hidden reservoirs.

"Slow down, please."

He silently refused until he stopped at the main road.

"I knew that was a bad idea."

She didn't answer.

"I don't blame you," he said. "I'm sorry."

Holden clicked on the radio to cover up the awful tension between them.

He turned north, away from Rio Madre, and drove toward Pismo Beach. She didn't object.

On the ride, the moon chased her, reflected against the dark lull of the ocean. She could see the two piers off in the distance at Avila, and a third closer to a controversial nuclear power plant.

"Kevin's right. I should be doing more. I know that," Holden said.

"He feels left out or jealous, I think."

"He never wanted me around the farm. He's always blamed me for our father leaving."

Passing the beach clubs and sandy stores close to the waterfront, he pulled into the parking lot in front of the Pismo Beach Pier.

Stepping onto the large slabs of wood, she stopped to watch the tiny breakers. She forgot where she was when he pressed his lips near her ear. "I love you."

"I know."

She studied his profile, but it revealed little, as if he had not spoken and were only thinking about the salty chill in the air and not her chilly response.

In the middle of the pier, several people were watching a

young man who had hooked something that bent his pole in half before he gave it more line.

"A pretty big fish," someone said.

"It may be a shark," said an old, unshaven fisherman with a gray hat.

They stopped to watch.

"Don't let him wrap the line around the pillar or he'll be tied down there to die," the gray-hatted old man said. "Don't rush."

The young man started to walk back and forth along the railing as several fishermen cleared out of his way. Probably eighteen or nineteen, the young man gracefully held his arms out. Several times the fish pulled the pole in half. He brought it to his chest as the creature fought for its life in a hysterical, desperate circle.

Moving closer to the railing, Kristin followed Holden's gaze down to two scaly silver fish, floating stiff and still in a half-filled bucket.

A small crowd gathered, clamoring and giving encouragement to the young fisherman, who didn't seem to hear anything, his face registering only determination to reel in the big one. Stopping and tugging the line, he stood still. She knew why when she saw the broken line that he waved for everyone to sigh at.

"He got wrapped around the pier," the gray-hatted old man said.

Kristin and Holden strolled away from the murmuring, disappointed crowd and didn't stop until they were at the end of the pier.

She turned back to the small group still gathered around the young man, consoling him and joking about the big one that got away. The cars were silent and appeared tiny, traveling down Highway 101. Civilization seemed distant.

Sliding toward the ocean, she gripped the rail, bending her head down to the black haze swishing against the pillars.

"I have some money saved that could help you get professional help, if you wanted to do that," Holden said.

"I can't think about that right now," she said.

When it became too cold, they walked arm in arm past the teenage fisherman, who now sat in a beach chair. His pole leaned against the rail with a new line in the water.

When they reached her father's house, they sat in the car beneath the streetlight that splashed down on the windshield.

Too restless to leave one another, they strolled down the block and crossed the street to St. Mary's.

"We're opposites," she said.

"Except we both lost everything."

In the middle of the night, she dreamed she was biting into a thick rubber tube or telephone wire. A surge of electricity buzzed through it. She could not quite cut through the rubber, but she knew she had discovered a source of power that was there for her to tap.

When the dream woke her, she had to wipe an extraordinarily thick amount of sleep from both of her eyes. It was then that she sensed something in the darkness, something she was unafraid of—a protector or guardian angel. When the phone rang, she lost awareness of what it was by her bedside.

It was an early call, and she rose to answer it. She thought it would be the substitute service as she tied her robe and picked up the phone.

It was Ms. Helms. "I think we should talk this afternoon."

Her cool, controlled voice gave Kristin the impression that Holden had spoken to her the previous evening.

Setting the time and place, Ms. Helms hung up.

At noon, Kristin parked outside the Rio Madre Inn, a throwback to the past where Frank Sinatra, Bing Crosby, and others stayed when they traveled from Los Angeles to San Francisco. Inside, the hostess wrote something on her pad and then pointed at Kristin with her pencil.

"Ms. Helms?"

"Yes."

Kristin followed her through the noisy buffet room toward the blue umbrellas outdoors, but the hostess guided her toward an exit sign where she imagined was another room. The hostess stopped, and she saw Ms. Helms sitting in a lone private booth.

The hostess grinned. "Enjoy your lunch."

Ms. Helms's firm grip surprised Kristin; she recalled the limp hand she had been given at the mall. The alert and kind eyes were the same deep green Holden's were in the sun. She slipped in across the table.

Kristin sipped her water while a busboy poured Ms. Helms's

glass. When he exited, Ms. Helms raised her head and blinked like an owl.

"I know what happened to you."

"I suppose if I had someone I trusted, I'd tell them everything, too."

"Frankly, I've never seen Holden this crazy about anyone before."

Ms. Helms's eyes softened, and she remained silent for a beat. Kristin had the feeling she had disrupted the script Ms. Helms had in mind.

"Do you love Holden?"

"I might."

"He loves you." Ms. Helms brought her hands together as if she were praying.

Kristin removed hers off the table so the unfazed woman would not see her rub them.

"He's a complex boy. An elite athlete. Brave. Insecure. A sensitive nature. And a real vicious streak at times. And handsome. He looks just like his grandfather, who was a ladies' man and fought in the Korean War."

Kristin believed the present often repeated or reflected the past, exposing patterns in our lives.

"I've loved that boy for more than twenty-eight years, and that includes the time I had him inside of me and loved him more than myself, which I still do."

"I can see how a mother would love a child so strongly, especially a beautiful boy like Holden."

Ms. Helms paused and squinted at her as if to see what she was made of. Kristin didn't know if these pauses were part of her normal personality, but she didn't think so, sensing that Ms. Helms was balanced on a precipice as steep as her own.

Taking a deep breath, Ms. Helms unfolded her hands. "I am truly impressed by your bravery and ability to survive what happened to you. Positive things come out of situations like this. My wayward son is alive again. That's something I'm very happy about." Ms. Helms lifted a shiny black purse, displaying displeasure before snapping it open and pulling out a check. "I want to help you." She laid the check on the table.

Kristin opened her mouth, but words kept spilling out from across the table.

"I was in a similar position when I was your age; my husband was a vicious alcoholic and several times put a gun to my head and threatened to shoot me." She slid the check across the beige tablecloth.

Kristin watched it slide closer—$25,000. "I can't accept this."

"I want to invest in you. It's not a handout. I believe in you."

She slid the check back across the table in one unhurried motion.

"I'm sorry," she said, "but—"

"I really respect you, and I don't think you should face this alone," Ms. Helms said. "I have a lot of money, but only one Holden, so you can see why I'm so concerned with someone he cares about so much." Ms. Helms sighed as if she understood her pain.

Kristin studied her up close. The gray power suit. Her smooth, natural complexion, requiring little makeup. Her hair black and thick. Ms. Helms bowed her head and Kristin caught a glimpse of a silver cross dangling outside her shirt.

"I don't know how to say this because I do care deeply about him, but he's way too close to me right now. I don't want to bring him down or take out my loss on him somehow and lose his love forever."

"What do you think you need to heal?"

"Some justice. Time. I don't know."

"You can go after him in a civil trial."

"I don't believe in the law. But I'm starting to believe in justice."

Outside, the sun dazzled Kristin for a moment and the wind blew hard in her face. A disheveled strip of long, black hair flew across Ms. Helms's cheek.

"I need to break it off with him. I can't be around him and find myself. I can't."

"He's going to be devastated."

"That's why I want to tell him right now. He's not ready, and I'm going from one extreme to another. It has nothing to do with him; he's too good to be true."

Ms. Helms squeezed both her arms, then wobbled away as if she had lost her equilibrium. "I just want my son back."

"I'm sorry."

Ms. Helms didn't turn around and jogged a little, making her hair tumble further down her shoulders.

An hour later, Kristin parked in front of the Helms Farms sales offices. It was silent except for the hollow sound of the wind, sending dusty shrubs across the valley.

Holden's pickup was under a palm tree, sunlight glaring off half the windshield.

"Hey, you're back!" Milo hurried down some stairs and veered toward her.

She walked faster to the porch.

"I'm talking to you." Milo cut her off and marched alongside her.

"Would you leave me alone?"

His thick hand gripped her arm.

"Let go of me."

He spun her around, forcing her to face him.

"You're too good to talk to me now? You need someone like me inside you. You have nothing inside you."

She pulled away. "You're a pig."

"What did you say?"

A pickup full of Mexican fieldworkers rolled up. She broke in front of the truck and sprinted to the house.

She turned around to see him stomp his feet and shout, "Keep your fucking mouth shut!"

She pushed open the front door.

"Holden?"

Realizing that she was not breathing, she managed an exhale. In the next room, she heard voices.

She knocked and pushed open the door.

Holden searched her face. "Hey," he said.

"I'll leave you two alone," Ms. Helms said.

"Are you all right?" he asked.

She wasn't sure she should say anything.

"Kristin?" Ms. Helms asked.

"Why is Milo always here, out front?"

"The sales offices are next door, upstairs."

"Did he say something to you?" Holden asked.

"We know how he is," Ms. Helms said.

"He threatened me."

"Stay with Mom."

"Holden?" Ms. Helms tried to stop him, but he was out the door. "Come back here! Holden!" his mother yelled.

Holden disappeared out the door.

"Milo's history. He's been a really devoted worker, but I can't overlook his antics anymore."

"He's done this before?"

"It's a lot of stuff."

Ms. Helms grabbed a phone. "Ed, Holden's headed toward the sales office, I think. You have to stop him. And get hold of Milo and tell him to go home and wait for my call." She hung up. "I can't look the other way every time Milo does something."

They ventured outside and where, from a distance, Kristin

saw Holden punch Milo in the neck and, amazingly, take a gun from him. Milo attacked like a bull, but Holden whacked him over the head with the gun, kicked him, and whacked him with the gun again. Milo's dark hair grew darker and red. His shirt was ripped, dusty, and bloody. Holden stood over him with the revolver and pulled the trigger. The gunshot rang and, as if taken by the wind, kept traveling through the flatlands and fields. Milo panicked, hitting his head against the building. Holden had missed him on purpose.

"You crazy fucking lunatic. I wasn't going to use it." Milo sat on his ass. He peered at Kristin. His eyes seemed to see her for the first time.

Ms. Helms demanded Holden hand her the revolver. "Where the hell did you get this?"

"It's his. Ask him." Holden nodded at Milo.

"Stupid, Milo. Stupid." Ms. Helms said.

"I'm going to sue you. I'm taking this farm."

"We know too much about you for you to do that."

"I'll press charges."

"You're the one with the gun, asshole," Holden said.

"Linda, I think you should hear my side before you take sides."

"Shut up." Holden kicked Milo in the face.

"Holden!"

Holden backed off with his hands in the air.

"Go home, Milo."

Milo kneeled and glared at Ms. Helms.

"We're through, Milo." Ms. Helms unloaded the gun.

"You're going to regret this." Milo spat out a gob of blood.

"We'll see you in court." Ms. Helms turned around and swept her hands in the opposite direction. "Everyone, let's get back to work. It's over."

A number of farmworkers, mechanics, and office workers who had appeared started to scatter.

Ms. Helms eyed Holden. "And I want to see you inside."

It was a sleepless night. The drama kept Kristin from speaking to Holden, but it also confirmed her understanding that she needed some time away from him. She called and asked him to meet her at a coffee shop, where they did not order coffee.

"I'm going to move to Santa Barbara, Holden. I'm sorry. I truly am." She turned toward her car. "It's not you."

"You'll only be a half-hour away."

"It's important for me to come through this."

"We've come so far."

"Not far enough."

"I want to give you all the space you need...but don't shut me out completely."

"I don't have a choice. I'm attracting the worst energy. I can't ignore that." Kristin kissed Holden on the cheek. "I'm sorry." She rushed to her car.

Neither of them waved as she passed him.

The sun appeared omnipresent as she drove toward it to Santa Barbara to find an apartment.

Part II: Holden

VII

HOLDEN WAS SO DRUNK he was barely able to sit on the stool.

The tall cowboy bartender picked up the phone. "I'm going to call you a cab, Holden."

"I can drive."

"I can't let you do that."

Holden stumbled off the stool. A large man helped Holden to his feet.

"I know where he lives. I'll give him a ride home."

"Who the hell are you?" Holden tried to recognize the man.

The man helped him outside.

Holden suddenly realized who he was.

"I know you."

The man flung Holden against a 1960s pickup truck.

Milo hopped out of the truck with a baseball bat.

Holden was too drunk to run or fight, but he took a wild swing that only spun him around.

"Batter up," Milo swung and pummeled Holden across the back.

Holden buckled. Milo kneed Holden in the face, dropping him to the ground. Milo didn't stop pounding Holden with his fists and cowboy boots.

Inside the Helmses' home, twelve-year-old Holden listened to David Bowie in his room. Fourteen-year-old Kevin appeared.

"Turn that queer music off."

Kevin ripped the cassette out of the stereo and then slapped Holden twice. "You little fag, listening to your fag music. You gonna cry?"

Holden put the cassette back in. Kevin ejected it. Holden faced him. Kevin pushed him. Holden, with incredible speed, bounced on Kevin. He pounded his fists into Kevin's body, feeling the frailty of the ribs that he tried to crack.

Kevin whimpered and wrapped his arms around his waist.

When Kevin crumbled to the floor, Holden jumped up and kneed his face. The onslaught of fists overwhelmed Kevin.

Holden's knuckles began to hurt as he whacked his brother's head.

"Uncle. Stop! Holden!"

When his mother appeared, Holden backed off.

"Mom! Mom!" Kevin cried.

"Holden! For Christ's sake! What are you doing?"

She kneeled by Kevin and stared furiously at Holden.

Holden rode his bike, hauling more than fifty newspapers, delivering them, and collecting for his paper route. He opened and closed his sore right hand and examined his bruised knuckles.

He approached a large house, an oilman's home.

It had a huge boat and truck outside that blocked the view to the neighbors.

The oilman's wife let him in. Everything about her seemed to sag, from her face to her stomach to her ankles.

At the dinner table were three kids—one boy and two girls.

A few moments after Holden entered, the teenage daughter began screaming at the father.

"You don't give a damn! You're down at the lodge getting drunk every day!"

The oilman was a towering man who wore cowboy boots.

"Do something with us for once in your life!"

"I pay the bills!"

The oilman's thundering voice shook the house when he spoke, though it was his teenage daughter who screamed at him.

"You're supposed to be a father, goddamn it!"

The youngest daughter looked at Holden with buggy eyes that seemed to have been traumatized out of their sockets.

Holden wanted to run, but he waited as the wife dug in her purse for the payment she owed him.

"It's in here somewhere," the oilman's wife said.

As Holden waited, the oilman noticed him.

"I want the paper porched. If it's not, I'm going to shove your handlebars up your scrawny little ass."

"Goddamn you! You leave him alone."

The wife handed Holden a five-dollar bill.

He reached into his little cotton bag of change, but she pushed him gently toward the door.

"You keep it. Thank you, Holden," the wife said.

The oilman banged on the table. "Don't tip him."

"You run along now, Holden."

Holden stared coldly at the man. This infuriated the oilman.

"You little shit. I'll teach you some respect."

Holden was out the door before the oilman could come after him.

Holden could hear his father yelling in the other room. His mother screamed back.

Furniture and glass crashed down in the house. Holden just lay in his bed, unable to sleep.

The next day, a Ford Pinto rolled by and a man tossed a bundle of newspapers onto the sidewalk for Holden.

Holden dragged it onto a nearby baseball field. He sat and began to fold and rubber band each one. When he finished, they were ready to be hung off the handlebars and delivered. Holden lay on the grass, staring up at the omniscient blue sky.

Holden pedaled as if they weighed a ton. He tossed papers onto several lawns.

He came to the oilman's house. Holden was not sure what inspired him, but he flipped one onto the roof. It immediately lifted his gloom, and suddenly he tingled with the sense of being his own person. He flipped another one onto the roof. He had fifty-six houses on his route and flipped up what he had left, about fifty bundles, onto the roof.

He didn't make them all; four or five papers nested in trees or bushes.

The rest lay in no particular order on the roof. Holden was crying angry tears, hoping someone would try and stop him so he could show them that he wasn't to be messed around with— but no one did, and he pedaled away.

Seventeen years later, the oilman and Milo dumped a bloody, beaten Holden out of the truck into the same field where he used to start his paper route.

VIII

WHEN HOLDEN FIRST MET KRISTIN, her skeletal frame reminded him of pictures he'd seen of women in concentration camps during World War II. Her face hung long and gaunt. Her hair was shiny and straight, like a teenager's. Her powerful and strangely alluring frailness at his brother's wedding obsessed him. If she had not been dressed, he was sure he could have seen every bone in her body. She seemed like an alien, with shy, anxious, cautious manners. Her skin appeared to be a thin shield.

"I lost myself so long ago," she told him.

She was smarter than he was, he understood. She looked right through him sometimes; she seemed to be able to only see the truth. At first, her gaze did not rest on anything long, except the ground or the distance. Her chin often touched her flat chest.

Since the first day he saw her, he felt his emotions split into so many types of love: hopeful, romantic, compassionate, sensual, marital. He needed her.

When she told him the horrible, but vague, details of what had happened to her, he read a handful of books about rape. He thought her story was new, but she wasn't the first. Victims were often "anorexic, intuitive, and delusional." He imagined them falling through a long tunnel, far below the earth, far from their own selves.

Kristin sometimes lived in a world she called "Happy Land," she once told him. Nothing could hurt her in her "Happy Land." It was an imaginary world that only she controlled, just like her writing. He read about how they rarely trusted anyone and sometimes turned into promiscuous women who went from relationship to relationship, severing emotional ties after short periods. Some victims became manic-depressive recluses who shunned human contact.

It was not supposed to be like this. They were both close to thirty, both athletic. She was a college graduate, he had money. They could easily have been a couple of yuppies in the suburbs. His heart ached for the good life that they should have had.

Ever since Holden was a little boy, he felt plagued by an anxious foreboding. He always thought it was his parents' fault. He could still feel the electric, explosive rages at the dinner table or late at night, the sound of dishes or furniture smashing against the walls as he lay in the darkness and silence of his bedroom. His father barely acknowledged him. They looked at each other as if they were from partisan worlds. He didn't know why, but as far as he remembered, his father never hit his brother. Holden would get a belt whipping across his backside, but not often and not for long. It was just his mother who was beaten, usually after his old man had had too many drinks but hadn't passed out.

Holden believed his stress would leave with his father. It didn't. His father left, but Holden didn't feel different. He worried until his father's death that he would be back, and his brother was still around enough to remind him.

His brother was often gone, camping or at 4H or at the lake with one of his countless witless buddies. Holden didn't join any group except baseball, and stayed in his room, listening to David Bowie, Alice Cooper, Led Zeppelin, Joy Division, or any band that caught his teen imagination.

His relationship with Kevin remained nonexistent. They avoided each other.

Holden was a baseball star from his first at-bat at age five, in peewee league, when his sharp ground ball shot past the left fielder and he ran all the way home. He was a coach's dream—until they got to know him. He was underground and moody and several times was kicked off teams by coaches he disliked—which was most of them—often for no compelling reason. He just had a burning hatred of authority. His teammates liked him for the most part, though he was never one of the guys.

Everything about him seemed all right to others. He didn't think people realized that his aloofness represented as much dysfunction as it did.

He had baseball and all the ease and glory and attention that brought, but he was never part of a championship team. Not one championship. Every team was second place at best. He never had the character of a champion. He did have the talent, and that's all he ever had—potential. He even received votes for "Rookie of the Year" his first season in the majors. This was after an excellent couple of months in Double-A and an equally productive time in Triple-A.

He began to do cocaine daily his second season. He lost weight. He began to make errors in the field. His batting average dropped. He didn't even care that he was benched.

When he tested positive for cocaine in a not-so-random test by the league, it was the beginning of the end. He was let go the next year.

His anger turned inward, and he just surfed every day. The waves and ocean and the infinite horizon took him outside himself. At night, he lay depressed on the sofa and listened to music.

No longer being a baseball player never bothered him. Neither did the drug addiction, but he was tormented by his inability to trust or have a relationship with a woman. He had had a number of affairs, but they all ended badly. He couldn't open up to anyone. It was his greatest fear, an irrational fear. He had never really been in love, until he met Kristin.

Since Kristin left, six months earlier, he felt as if his life was over. He couldn't imagine her with anyone else; he couldn't imagine himself with anyone else. He would do anything to win her back.

Part III: Kristin and Holden

IX

BEHIND THE TENNIS CLUB CAFE, Kristin sipped lemonade beneath a blue canopy. On the other side, a group of men sat around one of the white tables.

"He shot him," the lean older man with his fingers interlocked behind his head said.

"No, no. He didn't shoot him."

"They bought him off."

"I heard it had something to do with money," the older man said, as if that explained it all.

"I would have done the same thing, for Christ's sake."

"He played for the Reds in '82. Helluva ballplayer."

She didn't realize there was gossip about her and Holden, but it was not surprising; it was a small town. And her new home, Santa Barbara, was next door. She walked out as far away from them as possible.

She sat on a bench near the courts and watched her bookstore co-worker and recent tennis partner, Jeff, finish his match. He clenched his fist in triumph after hitting a forehand winner. She thought he was losing, but he had evidently made a comeback. He approached her, his sweaty face brimming with eagerness. "Five-four in the third," he said. "One more."

The gossiping men obviously had heard her name or recognized her somehow.

After Jeff's opponent missed an easy sitter on match point, Jeff gathered his tennis gear and hurried through the gates and up the steps. At the top, he rolled his eyes. "I got lucky," he smiled. "Let me report it and we'll go out and celebrate."

Jeff groaned in the parking lot, walking with a slight limp. "I'm as tight as a drum. I must be getting old." He placed his ball bag in his rusty 1965 Mustang's trunk and searched through the sweatbands, headbands, shirts, shoes, racquets, and used tennis balls to find his wallet. Taking the trophy in his left fist, he slammed the trunk shut with his right. "How does Mexican food sound? Maybe the Acapulco?" His voice rose, full of enthusiasm. "They make the best margaritas in town."

"I'm sorry, Jeff. I can't. I need to clean the house and do all the things I haven't had time to do this week. If I have a drink, I'll never get anything accomplished."

"Just dinner, then. You have to eat," he argued. "We've brought home the gold," he added, as if that would entice her into changing her mind.

"I'm too tired."

"We'll have to come out with some of the others one night during the week."

The "others" were their co-workers at the bookstore. The salary paid for rent and food and not much else. Jeff seemed to accept the logic of rejection. Three long blocks up Moonlite Drive, she could see the small one-bedroom apartment she rented. Circling around to the side, he parked next to the roses that lined her front window.

"I'll walk you to the door," he said, jumping out of the car.

Stopping and peering into his kind face, she realized what a tall guy he was and how perfectly rowed his teeth were. The way he stooped reminded her of her father. She folded her arms over both her racquets, across her chest.

"Is there anything between us?" he asked, grinning down at her.

She glanced at the passing cars. "I think you're a great guy, and I want to be friends and play tennis with you, but..." She glanced away from the recently mowed lawn to his poised interest. She set her right hand over her heart. "I'm flattered. I'm really flattered, but there is someone else in my life."

"I thought so. I didn't think you were a hermit."

He was wrong. She had been living in solitude, going out only for work, yoga, walks, an occasional movie and tea, but mostly staying at home.

He took a deep breath before pulling his restless hands out of his pockets to massage his furrowed forehead. He stepped off the porch, making them the same height. "It's the kiss of death when a girl says she wants to be friends with you." His moodiness disappeared and he seemed almost energetic. "I read last week that the average person meets forty-five people during their lifetime that they might possibly marry. I think the odds are still pretty good for me."

She liked him more than she had at any other time. "You'll find one of the forty-five soon."

X

THE NEXT DAY, WHEN KRISTIN was walking home from work, her heart popped with loneliness. She shivered with longing toward the miasmic Pacific.

A shifting scent, perhaps roses mixed with the ocean, puzzled her. The fragrance seemed to hang throughout the Mission area.

She was only two miles from the beach and roses were everywhere, so the bouquet probably wasn't unusual for the area that time of year.

When she reached her white and yellow-trimmed apartment, the side door connected to hers squeaked open. She remembered then that she was supposed to take her eighty-year-old neighbor's trash and recycling out and set it on the curb.

She unlatched the back gate. "Hello."

Mrs. Ott hesitated and searched for her in the direction of their backyard palm tree. When she found Kristin, she lit up. Mrs. Ott wore a new flower print dress and her usual soft, rubbery-soled shoes.

"I knew you wouldn't forget." Mrs. Ott wagged her finger. "I've been waiting for you. I didn't see any lights on, so I didn't think you were home."

"How are you, Mrs. Ott? Is that a new dress you're wearing? It's pretty."

She pulled the green plastic bag out of the trashcan.

"My daughter-in-law picked it up for me," Mrs. Ott said, her hand shaking, brushing over her ribs. "It's nice to have, even if I won't be around too much longer."

"Don't say that. You're not going anywhere." Kristin dropped the half-filled bag on the curb.

When she returned, Mrs. Ott sniffed west. "It smells like heaven tonight, doesn't it?"

They both turned to the sea as if that would help them pinpoint where heaven came from.

"You've never smelled that before?"

"Only once or twice in my life."

Kristin stared at Mrs. Ott as if the old woman knew what its origin was. "It's the sea and your roses, maybe?"

"You're such a pretty girl. Someone will catch your heart soon."

A cheerful shrug forced itself out of Kristin as she felt the seasoned assurance the woman always emanated.

"It's just a matter of time."

When they finished chatting, Mrs. Ott waved her small, wrinkled hand goodnight and, appearing tiny, turned all the way around to pull her door shut.

Lingering on the porch, Kristin gazed up at the starless sky. She didn't believe she knew much about herself or the life she led, and as emptiness shivered through her body, she entered the house.

XI

THE PRODUCER HAD BEEN a ball of hate in her for so long. All she could do was hate when she was alone. She needed to move past the hate. That's what frustrated her the most. It now was her problem.

That week she had a dream she was fishing with Jack Nicholson and Faye Dunaway. She had caught a small fish and was holding it up to Dunaway. Nicholson leaned against the pier railing smiling in approval. It was the pier that Holden and she had walked on. The water shimmered in the moonlight. It was the clearest dream in her life. An amazing dream.

The heat blistered again the next week. It was as if the sun had moved closer to the earth, making the last few weeks of summer unbearable. She had not spoken to anyone outside of work since this heat wave began. The bookstore was kind of fun, but she felt much older than the crew. They were all nice, young liberals from the university. She blended in pretty well, but she had to move on soon.

She only worked in the bookstore because she loved books, and it was a place to be safely involved in the world. It would be nice to be doing something more challenging.

She didn't regret writing *Young Scott and Zelda* at all. They paid for their sins. So did she. Scott never, ever gave up. Neither did Zelda.

She reread her script. It was a great story, but it was not the only story she had to tell anymore. She thought she would visit Taron and ask to meet her friend soon.

After work, she hiked along the trail below the overhanging houses until she climbed down a cliff to the boulders of moistly packed dirt to sit in front of Indian carvings and dangle her feet above the water. The ocean was clear, and she could see a lone perch and a bright red Garibaldi feeding off the reef in the protected zone below.

Everywhere she went, she began to see or think of Holden.

When the weather cooled, she ran on the beach. She could feel her cheekbones and tender areas around her eyes, and she remembered she used to have this focused feeling when she was a virgin in high school, and there was sex wanting to break out of her like there was then, too. It was becoming harder and harder to ignore. She needed love. Loneliness was making her either weaker or wiser. She couldn't tell anymore.

That night her father took her out to dinner.

"You've always been a good daughter," he said.

Potential problems were so easy to ignore when she was a child, he admitted. She was so quiet and well-behaved, and he was very proud, thinking she was turning out fine because she made good grades and the teachers and students liked her. He saw later the harm caused by living with him—being left alone while he was at work or at night when he fell asleep early every evening. It scared him, and he prayed that she would meet a nice boy and be taken care of.

When she left for college, he never expected her to come back. He didn't blame her. He believed she had experienced too much of his malaise already. She never had a clue he thought this, but he wanted to be honest regardless of how much it hurt, and he would not let her placate him or put herself down.

"Let me be honest," he said. "Don't give up like I did."

She went to the museum during her lunch hour twice the next week, to see the new show by an artist who wove twigs into little cages with bird perches in them, but with no way for birds to get inside. There were all sorts of wonderful, primitive, perfect, complex, and simple constructions. He shaped seven-foot-long solid yellow-gold tubes of bamboo as if they were in an arc of flight against the white walls. In the large room were bulky pieces of wood that looked as immovable as redwood stumps. She did not know how much this show affected her until she realized how strongly it still remained in her.

Something in her was nervously aware of Holden's presence. Someone fitting his description had come into the bookstore and asked when she worked. The clerk couldn't really remember anything he said, except that he was nice.

She knew what she needed to do, and called him. He agreed with her idea. It was the only way she could move on.

XII

SHE WALKED DOWNTOWN in the bright streetlights and headlights from the bumper-to-bumper traffic that rolled back from a traffic jam. Blinking at the luminous street, she turned the corner into Holden's pensive expression.

"Hi."

"Hi."

Her mouth became dry and she took a small breath as the cars crawled forward.

They veered off State Street toward a park.

She focused and saw him for the first time. He was shorter than she recalled, reminding her of a famous Italian or French film director. His forehead was high and his hair was cropped short. He was slender and fit; he had lost weight.

A new reserved intelligence resonated in him. Color deserted his face. "Do you want to talk about it?"

"Let's walk for a bit," she said. Her words sounded syncopated, reflecting her steps.

"Did you notice that fragrance the other night?" he asked.

"That was beautiful."

"I thought it had something to do with us."

In the park, the sky seemed to spin, making her feel dizzy, and she placed her cheek against a huge magnolia tree.

"My truck's not too far," Holden suggested, resting his hand on the magnolia's milky-smooth trunk.

All the pain and loneliness inside her focused on him. "You've changed," she said.

"In some ways." An enigmatic smile crossed his lips. "I almost didn't recognize you."

She had been working out regularly and had gained twenty-five pounds. She had breasts again.

She didn't say anything and started to walk, leading him to her home. Inside, she turned on the front room lamp, which she left on at night because she did not like to sleep in the dark.

"I want to do this."

"Okay."

He leaned in the doorway, silhouetting the light.

She took the stainless-steel handgun, a Ruger SP101, from him. She held it. "It's heavier than I remember."

"It's a powerful little gun."

"A .357 will knock down a strong man?"

"A .357 will stop an NFL linebacker."

At the Century City Mall in LA the next day, Kristin tried on a lovely white blouse. She checked how she looked in the mirror. Taron stood alongside her.

"You don't have a white shirt?"

"I don't."

"Sold."

Taron and Kristin hugged.

"I am so happy to see you looking so amazing."

"Thank you. Thank you for everything."

"I wish you could spend the night."

"Any other night."

Kristin passed by the producer's home. She stared at the top floor where his office was. A light was on.

Inside a pancake restaurant, Kristin sat in a booth and drank a glass of orange juice. In a booth further down, she could see Holden, wearing a black baseball cap.

She got up and went into the restroom. She splashed water on her face, and then bent down and gripped her stomach. She eventually stood and opened her purse. She took out the gun. She put it back in and walked out to her car. Holden had left.

She and Holden stood silently as the elevator took them up to the producer's office.

Holden backed off, out of view. Kristin knocked. No answer.

She put her ear against the door, but she didn't hear anything. She knocked harder.

She was ready to leave when the door cracked open. It was still chained. He peeked out.

He focused on her, trying to figure out who she was.

Recognition flashed across his face.

"Jesus. What are you doing here?"

"I don't know."

"What do you want?"

He tried to look to see if Kristin was alone.

"I want closure."

He unlatched the door. When he did, Holden kicked it open.

"Sit down and shut up." Holden ran around to see if anyone else was there.

The office was bare—no movie posters on the walls, no desk, and no bar.

Kristin aimed the gun at him.

"It looks like you brought a couple friends."

Kristin glanced at the closet where he had once put her.

"Did you come to kill me?"

His gaunt complexion was spotted with what looked like skin cancer. His hair was frizzier. He seemed almost scrawny.

Holden shoved him onto his leather sofa.

Kristin remained standing, with the gun aimed on him. "Maybe."

"I have money. How much will give you closure?"

"Have you done it to anyone else?"

He examined her, but didn't say anything.

Kristin aimed the gun at his balls. "You should have stopped when I said no."

"It hasn't been easy for me, either."

Her trigger hand trembled. "It hasn't been easy for you? I'm in. I'm in, in every fucking way! I walk around with my face and mind all locked up."

"I have prostate cancer."

"Who gives a fuck about you?"

"No one."

Kristin's skin vibrated with hate.

"I'll be dead by the end of this year." He stared directly at her. His right eye had almost completely shut.

Kristin pulled the trigger, but at the last second, she aimed at the couch.

He jumped and held his heart, turning toward the bullet hole in the sofa.

"Get up," Holden said.

The producer just stared at her with his one open eye.

Holden punched his other eye.

"Get up."

The producer stood and raised his arms. "I'm up."

"Get in that fucking closet," Kristin said.

"I'm sorry. I'm terribly sorry."

"Shut up." Holden hit him in the back of his head.

He fell to his knees.

"Get in the fucking closet," Holden said.

The producer crawled into the closet.

"Sit in the corner," she said. "Now."

"Do you want me to kill him?" Holden asked.

"No."

Kristin aimed the gun at the producer's head and pulled the

trigger. She thought there would be more blood. The producer lay motionless in the left corner of the closet.

Holden pushed the door shut.

Holden stood at her side. "He won't bother you again."

She contemplated Holden's words.

"You good?"

"I'm done."

The next morning, she recognized Mrs. Ott's fluff of white hair above the curtains on her back door. When she opened it, the woman's eyes beamed with eagerness. "I brought you over a surprise," Mrs. Ott said. She extended her arm and closed hand.

Kristin didn't take whatever she had.

"Go on, take it." Mrs. Ott opened her hand over hers and out popped a lovely diamond ring.

"This is real, isn't it? I can't accept this."

"Twenty-fifth wedding anniversary, and yes, you can. I had a dream of you wearing it, so you can't say no."

Declining to sit down, Mrs. Ott leaned back against the railing. "I don't need it. I've had people who loved me," she said, squinting up at the pale blue sky. "A career I cared about. I raised three healthy children, survived their crises," she chuckled. "I've had a full life. I've had enough."

After Mrs. Ott left, Kristin felt claustrophobic, so she changed into running clothes and went for a jog.

Normally she ran two miles, but she didn't seem to be tiring, so she hustled up and down hills, through mazes of quiet neighborhoods, the deserted college, parks, and down the southern beaches.

Her heart and mind were vacant, and she walked for a mile, relishing a pleasant exhaustion and fitness of pushing herself farther than she had ever gone.

That evening, she peeked through her drapes and saw Holden holding a painting or picture frame wrapped in brown paper in one hand and bottles of red and white wine in the other.

She brushed over her skirt and white shirt unnecessarily before letting him in. She stood flat-footed and said hello. They both made tiny, hesitant gestures before she moved halfway behind the door to give him space to enter.

"What's this?"

"I've brought you a gift. Go ahead—open it."

She tore off the paper and pulled it out.

"Are you ready?"

She flipped it around. The 16" by 20" photo was surrounded by a black frame and white mat. Largest and closest in perspective was her silhouette poised at the wishing well at the beautiful Santa Barbara Mission. Holden had signed the photo.

"You have great taste and a great eye, you know that?"

Pulling a small hammer out of his sport coat, he feigned a tap to her heart. "So, do you."

She watched him bang thin nails in the wall above the couch and align the photo.

She sat at the table and ran her index finger across a wine bottle's label. She glanced up at the photo "I need a minute."

She hugged her cramping stomach. When she could no longer hold in the pain, the tears burst. She had paid for the horror and sorrow of the past, she understood, and now she no longer felt its enslavement.

He kneeled next to her. "I love you."

"I feel as if we are connected." Her mind floated, a little dreamlike. "Everything is happening so fast."

His eyes following hers, the gravitational pull of hope brought them together. His mouth was warm as it met hers. She sank into him, softening.

Just before sunrise, she woke with the awareness of Holden outside the bed.

Holden hovered and stroked her hair.

"Holden?" She touched his cheek.

"Have you ever walked on water?"

"What?"

"Have you ever walked on water?"

"No."

"Meet me outside."

The sun had not risen, and the streetlights shone down on Holden's idling truck. In the pickup bed was a long surfboard and a smaller board.

Holden popped up from the opposite side of the truck.

"Is this how we're going to walk on water?"

"We're really going to do it."

Pulling off at a desolate exit, he rounded east between the stones and gold brush on the wide mountainside and the sun waking across a vineyard.

Holden carried and balanced the two boards on top of his head.

Long, small waves rolled across a long beach break.

Kristin listened as Holden gestured and discussed the surf.

Holden lay on his belly and popped up smoothly into a surfing stance. Kristin lay down and practiced with him.

Kristin pulled on a wetsuit he had brought for her. She attached the leash to her ankle.

"Ready?"

"I don't know."

"Stay relaxed. You can't do anything well unless you're relaxed."

Standing in the wet sand, she breathed in the early mist. The mellifluous morning ocean crashed and retreated to and from the shore, and it dawned on her that her roar and the hardness were now a memory. She soaked in the freedom and tiptoed in next to Holden. Goosebumps rose all over her.

Holden dove into the whitewater. Kristin jumped over so as not to get wet, but it was too late.

She flipped her hair out of the biting coldness. She hopped on the board and paddled.

"Heaven."

She swept her arm, splashing him. "It's cold."

"The first time is the most difficult. Don't be discouraged if you can't get up."

Holden was behind Kristin as she waited.

Kristin caught it and kneeled. She tried to stand but leaned too far to the right and lost her balance.

She rose out of the ocean as if she'd been baptized. Her eyes were open, and she stared up at the waking sky.

"That was amazing."

Kristin tried again but pearled into the shallow water.

On her next attempt, she slipped into the rushing wave.

She caught the following one. She popped up and surged with her arms outspread and glided to the beach, sinking half-way in the shallows.

Holden had his arms in the air. He hurried to wrap them around her.

Later, they sat on a small, forgotten dock and watched the sun sparkle across the ocean.

Kristin felt privileged to be looking out across the morning. She knew, regardless of what she created with her future, it would be worth nothing if this joy were not part of it—that hint of nature, love, and God that made her whole.

Endnotes

Young Scott & Zelda and *Three A.M. are* works of fiction. They lay no claim to be the truth that one would expect from literary scholarship or a biography.

In addition to the novels of F. Scott Fitzgerald and Zelda Fitzgerald, below are research references for the direct or paraphrased quotes from stories, letters, diaries, biographies, and online articles.

Young Scott & Zelda

F. Scott Fitzgerald, *The Great Gatsby,* in *The Fitzgerald Reader* (New York: Scribners, 1963), 130, 238.

F. Scott Fitzgerald, *The Last Tycoon,* ed. Edmund Wilson (New York: Scribners, 1941), 163.

F. Scott Fitzgerald, *Babylon Revisited,* in *The Fitzgerald Reader* (New York: Scribners, 1963), 318.

F. Scott Fitzgerald, *This Side of Paradise* (New York: Scribners, 1920), 26, 113, 167, 209, 217, 236.

Arthur Mizener, ed., *Afternoon of an Author* (Princeton: Princeton University Library, 1957), 93.

Matthew Bruccoli, Margaret M. Duggan, ed., *Correspondence of F. Scott Fitzgerald* (New York: Random House, 1980), 38, 43, 53.

Zelda Fitzgerald, *Save Me the Waltz* (New York: Scribners, 1932), 30, 36, 57.

Nancy Milford, *Zelda: A Biography* (New York: Harper and Row, 1970), 34.

Matthew J. Bruccoli, Scottie Fitzgerald Smith, Joan P. Kerr, ed., *The Romantic Egoists* (New York, Scribners, 1974), 35.

F. Scott Fitzgerald, "May Day," in *Tales of the Jazz Age* (New York: Scribners, 1922), 97. 117.

Malcolm Cowley, "The Romance of Money," in *Three Novels of F. Scott Fitzgerald*, 12.

Andrew Turnbull, ed., *The Letters of F. Scott Fitzgerald* (New York: Scribners, 1963), 91.

F. Scott Fitzgerald, "The Sensible Thing" in *The Fitzgerald Reader*, 96, 97, 101, 102.

F. Scott Fitzgerald, *Tender Is the Night* (New York: Scribners, 1934), 184 and 51.

F. Scott Fitzgerald, *The Crack-Up*, ed. Edmund Wilson (New York: New Directions, 1936), 344.

F. Scott Fitzgerald, "The Diamond as Big as the Ritz," in *Tales of the Jazz Age*, 168.

John Kuehl, Jackson Bryer, ed., *Dear Scott/Dear Max The Fitzgerald-Perkins Correspondence* (New York: Scribners, 1971), 21.

F. Scott Fitzgerald, *The Crack-Up*, ed. Edmund Wilson (New York: New Directions, 1936), 69.

F. Scott Fitzgerald, "The Ice Palace," in *Flappers and Philosophers* (New York: Scribners, 1921), 57-58.

Three A.M.

F. Scott Fitzgerald, *Babylon Revisited and Other Stories* (New York: Scribner, 1960).

F. Scott Fitzgerald, Zelda Fitzgerald, *Dear Scott, Dearest Zelda: The Love Letters of F. Scott and Zelda Fitzgerald* (New York: Macmillan, 2003).

Sheilah Graham and Gerold Frank, *Beloved Infidel, The Education of a Woman* (New York: Henry Holt and Company, 1958).

Ernest Hemingway, *Selected Letters, 1917-1961*, edited by Ernest Hemingway, Carlos Baker (New York: Scribner, 1981).

Ernest Hemingway, *A Moveable Feast, The Restored Version* (New York: Scribner, 2009).

Matthew J. Bruccoli, *Some Sort of Epic Grandeur: The Life of F. Scott Fitzgerald,* 2nd rev. ed. (Columbia: University of South Carolina Press, 2002).

Sally Cline, *Zelda Fitzgerald: Her Voice in Paradise* (New York: Arcade Publishing, 2002).

Andre Le Vot, *F. Scott Fitzgerald: A Biography* (New York: Doubleday & Company, Inc., 1983).

Sara Mayfield, *Exiles from Paradise: Zelda and Scott Fitzgerald* (New York: Delacorte Press, 1971).

Jeffrey Meyers, *Scott Fitzgerald: A Biography* (New York: HarperCollins, 2000).

Arthur Mizener, *The Far Side of Paradise: A Biography of F. Scott Fitzgerald* (Boston: Houghton Mifflin Company, 1951).

Nancy Milford, *Zelda: A Biography* (New York: Harper & Row, New York, 1970).

James R. Mellow, *Invented Lives: F. Scott & Zelda Fitzgerald* (Boston: Houghton Mifflin Company, 1984).

Kendall Taylor, *Sometimes Madness Is Wisdom: Zelda and Scott Fitzgerald, a Marriage* (New York: Ballantine Books, 2001).

Andrew Turnbill, *Scott Fitzgerald: A Biography* (New York: Grove Press, 1962).

www.ingramcontent.com/pod-product-compliance
Lightning Source LLC
Chambersburg PA
CBHW020654120726
47906CB00001B/261